Hanlon's Grazer

Book 10 of the Hugo Grazer Chronicles

Kevin W Cousins

ISBN-13: 9798423402358

CONTENTS

Hanlon's Grazer

Prologue: Waterhouse

The whirling sound of the whip was followed by crisp contact with skin. Four marks across her exposed back, the 12-year-old girl no longer cried out. She'd never met the tormenter prior to being shoved on the ground. As the rear of her dress was ripped open, she suspected that he was one of a dozen *lady prickers.*

"This witch shall brow justice," the average sized man claimed, grabbing the girl by the back of her neck. Yanking her from the muddy Essex Street, he turned to a coworker. "I suspecteth cater-cousins and neighbors of yond Francis girl art in league with the Beelzebub. Searcheth yon houses and dost not leave till thou findeth every beldam."

This man, wearing a breastplate over his leather kirtle, nodded then marched into one of the dwellings.

"Momma, Liz is nay witch," 15-year-old Joan Waterhouse said to Agnes. "Wherefore won't those gents leave her be."

It was July 13th, 1566, when the beaten girl was drug from the neighborhood. Joan Waterhouse and her mother could do nothing more than watch as British witch hunters ransacked the surrounding dwellings.

Joan's father had died of malaria seven years prior. He had once dedicated his life to the very magistrate that paid the witchfinder twenty shillings. With the authority of Parliament, the commissioned mob theoretically sought out those involved in witchcraft. The truth was that these men terrorized the community by rounding up Catholics, Jews, rumor-inflicted women, and others labeled heretic.

"Hush, child," Agnes told her daughter. She knew that most of the accused failed the witchfinder's tests. Being accused was always fatal. "Dost not speaketh. We might but giveth cause to believeth ill of us."

"Hark," claimed another *lady pricker*. He had come out of the Francis home to find the women conversing. "I insist thou cometh with us for questions."

"Prithee, Sir. Nay," pleaded Agnes but the man grasped her arm.

Holding her close to his filthy body, he demanded, "Take thy daughter, likewise. They may well be parteth of an issue of witchcraft."

As her mother was led away, a balding man approached Joan. He was a familiar face. A member of the neighborhood. She smiled up at Mr. Talbot. Her expression changed to panic as he snatched

Joan's left wrist. How could he voluntarily be part of the atrocity? She pleaded and pulled but Talbot could not be forced away. Her wrist ached as she was guided away. Once she stopped digging her heels in the mud and resisting, the pain to her arm subsided.

The sun was setting when the Waterhouse women joined the line of suspects. Nearby, people from all over Essex gathered to watch a blaze. Once a few accused had been moved from the front of the procession, Joan made out twenty long wood poles surrounded by timber skirts. Two had been lit. Liz Francis was being tied to one. Below her was mostly smoke and an occasional flicker of flame.

The glowing fragments from the larger blaze caused Joan to look away.

"Ealdemodor? Momma, tis Ealdemodor (Grandmother)!" yelled Joan.

"Perchance she hath failed ye test," suggested Talbot. "If thee and thy mother art decent folk then you'll not shareth such a fate.

"Pray thee, almighty," cried Agnes. "Mine own wretch of a mother slain."

Soon it was Agnes' turn to approach a man sitting in a wooden chair with a table between him and the accused. One look at his tricorn hat, made from wool, she knew he was the witchfinder. His expression was one of pompous indifference. He dipped his quill into ink then began to write as he spoke.

"Thine christened name?"

"Agnes Waterhouse, Master witchfinder."

"Residence?"

"Essex, sir. I hath dwelled yonder with mine daughter and mother."

"Test her," he ordered.

"Wherefore, master? What doth it matter? You'll killeth me likewise," she stated. "My mother didst faileth thy test. She wast a god-fearing mistress."

"What wast her name?"

"Wilmina. She's the poor soul thee burned first!"

"Dost thee doubt thee ability to passeth ye beldam test?"

"Mine daughter and I art god fearing distaff of this community. We wouldst never alloweth flibbertigibbet tools within our abode. If it be a true test, then we wouldst succeed."

"She's a witch," claimed the man holding Agnes. The witchfinder motioned for another *lady pricker* to come forward. The man carried a knife. "I hath heard thee necromancer whispering to yond welp."

The knifeman turned one last time to the

witchfinder and, seeing him shrug, brought the blade across Agnes' arm. Blood trickled from the small cut.

"Grammarcy for thy earnestness, Mistress Waterhouse" he said. On another sheet, he jotted down her mother's name. Joan was tested with the same result. Seeing the begrudging expression on the man behind Agnes, the witchfinder questioned him. "Morcant, didst thee observe dame or lady Waterhouse conversing with Lucifer, imp, or other conjuring?"

"Uh. Aye," Morcant responded.

"Be warned," the witchfinder replied, setting down the feather-ended quill. "If thee sayeth thee witnessed a demonic aberration, I shall insist thee best ye maleficium test. I asketh thee again, what didst thee witness?"

"Nil, master," Morcant confessed. The tester returned his knife to its sheath. Upon close observation, Agnes saw the blade detract slightly. "Verily I hath heard thee Waterhouse's whisper."

"I see nil to detain mistress Waterhouse or progeny," the witchfinder declared as he stood. "Fare thee well."

"Hold, sir." argued Morcant.

Talbot smiled as he released Joan. The twitching

of facial muscles revealed his nervous feelings.

"Mine own decision is final. The test hath been bested," the witchfinder stated with a glare toward Morcant. A nonverbal threat passed between them and the *lady pricker* understood its meaning. He stepped away from both women, merging with the crowd.

"Cometh now, daughter," Agnes insisted. Holding hands, the mother marched young Joan through the gathering.

"Witch! Filthy beldams!" Villagers chanted from random areas.

"Stop the hags!" It was Morcant's voice.

"The witchfinder hath found us innocent. Wherefore art we in such haste?" Joan inquired. She breathed heavy while holding up a section of dress. This was the technique the women used when wading through ankle deep sections of mud. "Momma. Wherefore didn't those gents save ealdemodor from the fireth?"

"For the reasoneth they shall apace changeth their mind about us, daughter. They care not for justice. Once the mob gathers, it wanteth nothing less than flesh and blood."

"Such response maketh little reason, momma," Joan decided. She recognized her front door as

Agnes pulled her past. "Where doth we venture?"

"Afar," her mother replied.

Their trek took them a dozen cottages along the street before a calloused hand clamped onto Agnes' slender neck. Though oxygen was constricted, and vision blurred, there was no doubt that the fat fist belonged to Morcant. His breath burned her nostrils as her grip with Joan loosened.

"Dost refrain from running to thy dark master, beldam," Morcant stated. "He'll see thee lief enow."

Preoccupied with her mother, Joan trudged away. She took refuge behind a group of barrels next to a carriage house.

Dropping Agnes in the mud, the *lady pricker* scanned for her daughter. Arriving villagers brought his attention back to Agnes.

"This one talks to the flibbertigibbet. She needeth silenced ere her demonic influenceth spreads throughout Laingaham, Essex, and the whole of Britain."

From the gatherers, a pebble shot forth. It struck Agnes' bonnet, causing her to wince. Her mouth opened to speak but the voice was drowned out by chants.

"Witch! Beldam! Heretic! Necromancer!"

The labels were followed by a barrage of

projectiles. One fist-sized chunk of granite struck Agnes Waterhouse in the nose.

"Prithee, nay," she pleaded. Her hand covered the blood-soaked nose as more rocks accosted her.

Joan saw little of the stoning from her safe place. Her mother's fate was discovered after the crowd thinned back toward the public burning.

Finding her mother's still form in the street, the daughter dropped to her knees. The bloody face of Agnes stared up with motionless eyes. Joan cried as she lay over her mother. Shaking, she looked up to see a few neighbors had returned. Fear gripped her then she got to her feet and strolled away.

Tired limbs took her into the wilderness as her senses tried to detect the accusations that proceeded the death mob. When she came to a spot void of cottages, or other manmade objects, her frame slowed to a stop. With her rear propped against a tree northwest of the village, the young girl crouched. Tears formed as she taxed her lungs. The harsh exhaling roared in her ears while her eyes focused on the state of her clothes. A feeling of sweaty lethargy made her oblivious to the men positioned barely ten yards away.

"'Tis grand yond witchfinder posted us hither, Rionet."

Looking to her left, Joan discovered two rough looking characters with thick, worn attire. She knew the look of paid soldiers. The one on horseback continued to speak as he dismounted.

"Free from justice, this wretch may well have spread her bedlam throughout Essex."

"Lop off her head, Jolis!" Rionet held the horse's reigns as Jolis unsheathed a three-foot sword. "Dost not permit her an audience with Beelzebub."

"I'll make it quick, Rionet," Jolis assured his comrade as he approached the screaming girl. As the blade raised, Joan but her pale palms together and closed her eyes.

Expecting death, she was shocked when her left wrist was grasped. Moved from the tree, Joan assumed the soldier had wanted a better vantage point to cleaver her to pieces. The girl was too tired to resist.

When she heard Rionet's voice again, it sounded a distance from her. "Get ye back, imps of lucifer!"

Her lashes lifted, showing both soldier's next to the horse. In a crescent, from left then behind to the right, where more people. The newcomers wore straight moss toned robes which flowered at the bottom. If not for breasts, they resembled tapered handbells. Beneath each hood, features were obscured by wood masks with a dark chunk of rock embedded on the forehead.

"Thine soulless issue tis witchfinder property and ye almighty!" declared Jolis.

The figure to Joan's right responded.

"Thy world is not wholly noble, sir. Henceforth, thee shall be left to the peril of thee victims."

Rionet blinked, repeating the motion a few times before forcing his eyes to squint. The sword pointed to Earth as though gesturing defeat. Abruptly he thrust the blade into the air, made slicing motions before returning the tip to the weeds.

"Where art thou?" he questioned.

"The lights from the village," claimed Jolis. "Yea the moon tis gone."

The 15-year-old survivor looked up to see lunar luminescence poking from between branches. Watching the men stumble off into the moonlit forest, the girl realized that the wooden faced woman had somehow blinded both.

"What is thy name, issue?" her protector asked, crouching down to eye level.

"Joan Waterhouse," the girl smiled. The hand carved mask was removed. An angelic face greeted her with a warm grin. "What is thy name?"

"Brynhild Margarita Aelfweard," the woman replied. This was followed by introducing her companions. "Thy child shall journey with thee."

Joan, having no living family, felt good about the idea. She considered her response as the others came to her side. The start of a word was cut off by the woman introduced as Sorcha Jane Kaenylm. She had tossed an old sack over Joan's head. The fabric slid along her arms, below the hips then the child's world flipped. She tried to call out as her body tumbled to the bottom, but the outside world was unconcerned. With the opening tied, the bundle was slung over a shoulder. She felt every bump as she was carried like a sack of soiled clothing.

"Who art thou?"

"We art the wholly threat that yond men detest," Brynhild confessed. "Ye, little Joan, art the innocent thee were meant to protect."

"But," the captive insisted. "Ye were pleasant."

The group laughed.

"Mayhap," the witch introduced as Sorcha giggled. "Only because thee hast yet to spread our influence."

Joan, due to exhaustion, did not struggle. Instead, she wept until sleep took her.

Her waking hours were filled with beatings,

verbal abuse, and harassment. Days passed before she was cleaned up and taken to an unfamiliar area within the stronghold. Most of the rooms she'd seen during her captivity were built from cut logs and lit with hooded candles. This room, with rugs covering the hard flooring, was designed to highlight a centralized, throne shaped tree. Rear branches arched up from the chair backing, reaching twelve feet up and spreading out to form the ceiling. The child could see that the tree also formed the wall supports.

Upon the throne seat sat another angelic woman. Joan felt that this one dressed more like a woman of breeding. Had she come to take her back to civilization? In her hand, the woman perused a tome with weathered pages. Its cover was dark and hard to see. The child did see the pages the woman was viewing. They were handwritten in Latin accompanied by drawings. In the upper corner of a page was the sketch of a witch's mask. A drawn line pointed to the rock above the eye openings. It was labeled 'Black tourmaline crystal: used for protection against lower vis enchantments.'

"Thy presume thee hast been adequately accommodated," the well-dressed woman inquired. Her eyes stuck to the page until an utterance formed on Joan's lips. The woman's index finger came up, indicating that Joan should not speak. "Thy art the great witch Una Crina Dacian."

"Una," blurted Joan.

Brynhild Aelfweard's hand smacked the child's face. "Thee shalt not speaketh until thy mistress hast concluded. Likewise, thee addresseth thy master as the great witch, the one, or Mistress Dacian. Nil other."

"Ye shall forthwith refer to yon sisters as empusa followed by first nameth. Hast Empusa Brynhild explained thy purpose?" After a motion from Joan, the great witch continued. Her voice was strong and clear. "Thee hast arrived at our wilderness abode as ye candidate to replenish ye fallen sister, Empusa Magisend."

Though quietly listening as Dacian explained, the news made the young captive ill inside.

Chapter One: Damn Skippy

Other than my own account, the entries from this progress journal make up a guideline for what will be put in the Profanus Files *Ewai90* and *Harpia90*. I often rely on hearsay, witness accounts (human, ghost, etc.), and read material (sources including Tools for Practical Witchcraft, and Cadadrius files) to fill in the blanks. Events may not be a hundred percent accurate. For example, if I weren't there, I couldn't know words used verbatim. This record is strictly for my reference of the probable order of events.

Hugo A. Grazer July 17, 1992

"Becca," I pined, sitting with my arms against the bay window. Expecting it to be cold, my forehead made contact with the glass. Feeling a temperature in the low sixties, I backed away.

There was a cherry car parked at the curb, on the other side of the street, near the side entrance of the eight story Tokeca Hotel. That red and tan brick structure was the oldest in town, built along Mississippi Drive in 1914.

I was visualizing the two women that had exited the vehicle. The driver looked familiar but my brain, still sluggish from the late-night drinking, couldn't identified her. Though she'd done something with her hair, the other was definitely Becca Webb.

A spectral form had been watching from the other side of the room. I picked up my notebook and started playing with writing another profanes file. I suppose that's when ghostly Garius decided to fade back into the mirror.

"October 7, 1990," I read as I jotted it onto paper. "No. That's today's date. It should be the date of the encounter. What monstrum do I want to talk about? There was that stone guy or the gelatinous blobby thing. This isn't going well. I can't stop thinking about Becca."

Setting the notebook and pen on the carpet, I get up and got dressed for the day. Once my shoes were in place, an urge came over me.

"Leave well enough alone," I told myself yet, a moment later, I rushed for the apartment door. Running down the stairs, I knew where I was going but wasn't convinced of what I'd do or say when I arrived.

"Okay, God. If you're so great, why don't you help me with my love life?"

"Hugo?" I heard from over my shoulder. I'd barely gotten out the apartment building entrance and as far as a parking meter when she called to me. I turned and found exactly who I'd suspected. "I thought that was you."

"Colleen. Hey," I smirked. She looked great which made things worse in my head because it made her harder to resist. She stepped close as she spoke and, I'd swore that she was intentionally lifting and pointing her breasts at me. So much for God's help.

"It's so nice to see you," came her melodious voice with that accent that melted my insides. "It's been a while."

"Uh, yeah. It's great seeing you, Mrs. Kastleberg," I replied. I hoped using her formal name would keep her at a distance. The trouble was that I could smell her perfume and the scent of her hair. She was too close, and I was getting nervous. "I'm really in a hurry. See you around."

My feet moved swiftly across Iowa Avenue and into the hotel. I had no plan of what to do inside but desperately needed away from Colleen. The last time I'd seen her, she was bat crazy; carrying on about how I'd ruined her marriage and was cheating on her. The second part of that was correct. I'm not proud of myself but, after all her mental torment and blaming me for all her troubles, I needed someone to take me away from the anguish.

Before you judge, let me explain. I went over to her house one afternoon to find her having sex with another guy. I'd like to say it was as cut and dry as her stepping out on me but we're dealing with a headcase. She claimed that the twenty something in her bed was Ranger Kastleberg. In reality, this guy could have graduated high school with me.

What do you say when your girlfriend tells you she's having an affair with her dead husband but still wants to be with you? I left, got really drunk, and ended up waking up with a woman I met at a bar.

Colleen took me back as though she were some sort of saint, but the incident got added to her arsenal of verbal attacks. Was I permitted to bring up the night she cheated on me? Nope. Any mention of the indiscretion caused her to go down the screwy squirrel hole. I finally smartened up and left her. It wasn't easy. When she wasn't a raving lunatic, Colleen was a caring, adorable human being. People who didn't know about her dark side thought we made the perfect couple. A part of me missed 'her' but there was no handling 'Kooky Colleen.'

"I wonder if her psychiatrist ever got her medication straightened," I said, stepping through the hotel lobby. The desk clerk was busy with an old couple and didn't notice me. In the dining area, I saw Becca at a far booth. Her dark hair was blonde, layered on the sides, with red highlights growing beneath her shoulders. The bangs were straight and extended to her brow line. She wore denim overalls which covered most of a white striped, short sleeve, shirt.

Her friend was slightly obscured as I sat on a

bar stool and ordered an orange juice. "Um, never mind. Put some vodka in there too."

Her friend came into view. The rubber band had been removed, exposing straight shoulder length hair. That smooth bronze complexion struck a chord in my memory. She was Wilona Schuster, one of the cheerleaders that used to pester me in high school. How do you forget a girl that constantly teased you with her body for the sole purpose of making you feel awful?

I suppose I shouldn't have been surprised to find her with Becca. They both traveled in the same social groups. My opinion of her was much higher. Why? What did I really know about Becca Webb?

"This was a bad idea," I decided as the bartender tried to strike up a conversation.

"Did you know that this hotel was the tallest building in town until 1970?" He pointed to a framed photo of the building. The lower caption read *Tokeca Hotel 100 Mississippi Drive.* "At its completion, it was also the most expensive."

I chugged my drink. Removed from the stool, I just wanted out of that place. I'd passed the arch separating the dining room with the lobby, around the quaint front desk, before spotting two brown doors. One had the simplistic emblem of a man.

"You can wait. It's just across the street," I told myself. Whether psychological or an actual need, there'd be no leaving before visiting the restroom. Using a full-length urinal, I admired the old-style tiles and century old porcelain. Some guy stepped up to the urinal next to mine and I realized their restroom would never compare to the one at home. It was private. After washing my hands, I passed to the other side of the door. I sighed with relief.

"Thought that was you," Wilona announced. I had hoped that she was talking to someone else, but her gaze was locked on me. "Hey, Becca! It's Grazer."

Becca, who was paying the bill, finished, and walked over. Though the strength of the vodka-Ergerteine mix made my body feel great, the women caused me to shake. Nervous, a part of me wished I'd stayed in the apartment.

"Did you see that guy that passed me?" Becca's pink lips asked. "He was hella creepy."

Beyond her was a man in a black trench coat. The perfectly groomed rear of his scalp reminded me of brown doll hair. Otherwise, he looked average.

"You two know each other, Willo?" Becca

asked. Her friendly voice cut through my awkwardness.

"Yeah," said Wilona Schuster as Becca placed a hand on her bare shoulder. I was cut off before I could contradict. It was too late. Becca's hazel glance was drowned out by a set of yellow-brown eyes that drew my attention like a cobra hypnotizing its next meal. The courage to 'out her' was gone. "We were great friends in school. I miss talking to you. How are things hanging these days?"

"Life is sweet. Maybe we could go to my place and catch up," I blurted.

It was a quarter till nine in the morning. They had to have seen me drinking at the bar. Then I invite them to my apartment? As though that didn't add up to being overly 'pervy' with one woman, the situation came across like I'd propositioned both. I couldn't shake their time-stopping eyebeams. It felt like Becca was reading the inside of my skull, checking every thought except what I wanted her to see.

"Your crib? Actually," replied Becca. "Willo and I were headed to the arboretum."

"We have an arboretum in town?" I inquired.

"Sure, behind the Discover Nature Park. We wanted to check out the crazy tree everyone's been talking about," added Wilona. Her light blue jersey was snug against her body. With the numbers 01 on the front, it made it impossible to forget she had once been a cheerleader. "You should come along."

"In your own car, Hugo," Becca added. "We're having a girl's day. You understand."

"Sure," I responded. "Maybe another time."

"I didn't mean it that way," she insisted. "We want you with us at the arboretum. It's just that we have an appointment, later, at the nail salon.

"I'm looking forward to a pedicure on top of all the fingernail pampering," explained Wilona.

"Aiight! Afterward it'll be clothes shopping," said Becca.

"I'm getting the picture. Hiking to look at trees, yes. Shopping and nail painting, no." It was fine. I was interested in the shiny coin but not how it was minted. Does that make any sense?

"You don't think my nails could use a little color?" I joked.

"You never seemed like the type of man that swung that way," Wilona replied, lifting a brow.

"He doesn't," Becca interjected. It almost felt like both women were 'into me.' Even with my hyper ability to lie detect, I was blind to most signs that women were interested.

"No polish for this guy," I smiled, pointing both thumbs at myself.

After more joking, we agreed to meet at the stone that marked the separation between the Discover Nature Park and the arboretum.

"Got to bounce," said Wilona. She showed her back to me, looking physically fit in her bareback model jeans. The brown and silver Lawman logo showed over her right rear pocket as Becca added, "See you in twenty."

They assumed I had a vehicle, but my old Chevy Monza had broken down back in July of last year.

"I miss the white wonder car. It didn't drive the best, but women loved it," I said to myself. Stepping into the road, the old 2-door 'babe magnet' got me thinking of the times Colleen Kastleberg drove us places. "Stop thinking about that psycho."

Near the apartment building, my eyes caught a reflection in the *Prohibition Bar and Grill* window. Becca's stranger emerged from a reverse image of the hotel. I'd have guessed he was about six foot in height; wide shoulders got me to think the man was heavier than average and all muscle.

His head shifted, unnaturally, as he hobbled to the curb. Except for the hair, his backside had seemed normal enough; overcoat, khaki slacks, and business shoes.

Turning toward the street, its neck wobbled from side to side. Whatever his disability, it gave the stranger the appearance of a giant bobblehead. Another odd characteristic was the way the trench coat was held open at both upper pectoral muscles by bizarre broaches. The glassy discs reminded me of the lenses from those novelty spectacles. You know the ones. People used to wear them to look like they had super bad eyesight.

What about his eyes? They were without life, embedded in stiff, unmoving flesh. Webb was right. The pasty skinned man was creepy and unnerved me. Why was he there? Was he waiting for someone?

Another customer came from the hotel exit, causing the stranger to shuffle up the sidewalk. My eyes left his neck wobble for the movement of his arms. I noticed that there was a difference in tone.

"Why tan your hands and not your face?"

I considered the problem while entering the apartment stairwell. When I returned to the sidewalk, thoughts were limited to the time I had remaining.

Mounting the tall bike, I put my foam headphones over my ears, adjusted the plastic speaker headband, then tuned my AM/FM receiver on my belt. *Warrant* played *Cherry Pie* between static and station interference while my feet cranked the ten speed up Iowa Avenue's incline.

The morning vodka, mixed with Ergerteine biology, propelling me up Iowa to Fulliam Avenue, Houser Street, Cedar Street, and into the park. I'd traveled three miles, arriving at the large granite marker labeled *Tokeca Arboretum*, in ten minutes. I was five minutes shy of the meeting time.

Hoping I'd gotten there ahead of Wilona, I chained the bike to a birdhouse. One of the peddles was bent. I shouldn't have put that much pressure on the 10-speed but was anxious about the uphill riding. Enthusiasm pumped every ounce of strength into my legs. I really wanted to see Becca again. Or was I interested in Wilona? "Dude, you have problems."

Dashing to the slab of stone, I found them waiting. Wilona's Toyota MR2 was parked a short distance away.

"OMG, Hugo," announced Becca. "You must

drive like a bat out of Hell. Willo was going at least ten miles over the speed limit."

"We did get slowed down by the transit bus," Wilona admitted as we began walking onto the southern of two paved trails. "By the way, we need to keep moving."

"Because of your appointment?" I asked.

"Damn skippy," Wilona admitted. "Also, the bus drops off sightseers. They'll be here soon."

Every tree was spread out in a row with its identification marked on signs. We knew, briskly walking, when we'd passed a horse chestnut, sugar maple, eastern wahoo, chinkapin oak, bigtooth aspen, or others in the accessible area. Pleasant weather plus spectacular fall colors made the event enjoyable. Until that day, I couldn't imagine strolling along, gawk at trees, would be much fun.

The pavement went south, curving into a nine-hundred-foot J, then forking at a wood line. Each of three splits were formed from dirt with intermittent sections of brick or wood. Wilona took the far western trail. Ten feet from the start, they found a marker for *Nyssa sylvatica Black gum trees.* Three trees populated both sides of the path.

"Wow. The leaves are so red," I admitted. "They almost glow."

"Makes sense that you'd favor red, Demon killer," grinned Wilona.

"As if," was my response. This area was no longer like the open fields we'd passed. The arboretum had become dense with overgrowth. "Whoever started that rumor doesn't know me."

"Sure. We should call you Occam Grazer," Wilona giggled.

"Isn't Occam's Razor something like 'the simplest answer is usually correct'?" I questioned. "Are you calling me simple?"

"No, but it fits your name," she insisted. "Grazer. Razor."

"Like Newton's Flaming Grazer sword," Becca added. "Get it. Grazer, laser."

"What are you, a couple of science geeks?" I kidded.

Chapter Two: Murphy's Law

Having spent that morning with Wilona Schuster and Becca Webb, my nervous jitters left. We laughed and talked like three old friends, people who'd spent a lifetime together.

"We were both top of our class in math and science," bragged Wilona. I nodded because I remembered their grades were the best in class.

"And still found time to have a dope social life," added Becca.

"I'm down with that," I said, trying to impress them with my street lingo. Their demeanor was that look you get after sucking on a lemon. "Anyway, if I have to be named after a philosophical principle, how about Hanlon's Razor?"

"I don't know that one," admitted Wilona while strolling past a small witch hazel tree. She smiled at its golden oval shaped leaves.

The land used for the arboretum and the Discover Nature Park had once belonged to a farmer. Much of it had been regrown from hay and cornfields. From the dense growth and huge trees, I suspected that we were walking through the original farm property.

"I know this one," Becca declared. "Never assume something is done for bad reasons if it can be explained by incompetence or stupidity."

"Not bad but Hugo seems more like a Murphy's Law guy," Wilona replied. "Anything that can go wrong."

"Will," added Becca. "I can see that. He always has that cloud following him."

"Cloud?" Her comment perplexed me. Did I have a specter or daemon clinging to me? I told myself to chill. She was talking about my personality; often looking at the negative. My level of thickheadedness surprised me sometimes.

I decided to go back to enjoying the moment. Becca stood under the limbs of colorful birch leaves. Looking over the huge plant, I was wishing I'd brought my camera when I noticed that stranger again. Standing in long grass, he was five yards on the other side of the birch trunk. He'd been stalking me.

Great, I thought. As though having an ex-girlfriend constantly spying on me wasn't enough. Was this guy dangerous? Would he hurt Becca or Wilona?

"Forgotten something at the car," I whispered, having stepped to Becca's side. "I'll be right back."

"Your car?" overheard Wilona. The women laughed and it was apparent that they knew I'd arrived via bicycle. "Whatever. Hurry back or you'll miss us at the yew tree."

"Yeah. I want to know what everyone's talking about," added Becca. I took a few steps north. "Maybe he left something in the glove box. I sure hope he didn't forget the combination."

I couldn't blame either for having a joke at my

expense. I'd been less than honest and got caught. I had become so guarded about aspects of my life that I found myself omitting the insignificant things. So, what if I did ride my bike everywhere? If they didn't like it then I shouldn't have anything to do with them. The reality was that I'd have happily kept lying if it meant spending more time with either.

Through tan grass, the stranger shuffled to the north. I doubted that he had followed me to the arboretum. The frozen state of his eyes convinced me that he had tunnel vision. That's when I decided that the transit bus had brought him there. As I headed back to the stone marker, the stalker was insistent about catching up. Being uncommonly warm for October, he was hindered by his outfit.

Ten yards from the start of the arboretum, I stopped to consider confronting the weird man. His head wobbled closer and, as he came within talking distance, something told me that kindness wasn't warranted.

Bolting across the groomed lawn to his left, I sprinted out of range. Back on the paved trail, my feet took me to the birch tree. Having a general idea of Becca and Wilona's destination, I took a shortcut through the woods. I'd barely gotten on a trail when the Ergerteine failed. It was worrisome. What if the stranger did mean me or my friends harm? Would I have a chance against him without my 'edge'?

Busy running scenarios through my brain, my foot caught one of the buried logs used as trail steps. I stumbled down the incline and over a wood plank. Finally, with my equilibrium in check, I noticed a six-foot-deep chasm. It wasn't wide but contained a flowing brook and a lot of rocks. At twenty-two, when the Ergerteine was dormant, healing wasn't a certainty. I'd been fortunate enough not to fall or I'd have been hurt badly, maybe killed.

I turned away and, oddly, tripped again. This time my foot discovered a tree root growing above the soil. I fell forward, onto my head. Lifting my mouth from the earth, I winced until enough dirt was free from my eyes. I spit out soil before realizing that I was in direct visual range of a tree trunk. Next to it was a white sign painted *Taxus Baccata, English Yew tree; Caution, leaves and berries are toxic.*

This yew was over forty foot in height with gnarled appendages reaching as much as eighteen feet from its wide base. I was at root level when I saw the perfectly carved fingers. The portrayal, from tip to lower arm pit, wasn't designed with any artistic method I'd ever seen. Bark covered much of it as naturally as the rest of the plant. Eight inches up from this piece began another sculpture. It displayed the point of a shoulder to a neck then a head with an expression of terror.

"Oh God," I bellowed. "That's. It looks like…"

"It does, right," I heard Becca say.

Wilona helped me from the ground. I brushed nature from my thick hair which I'd allowed to grow to the middle of my neck. I needed a trim because my mane had grown over most of my ears and the right cowlick just added to a permanent disheveled appearance.

"The artist got Murry Carrol's features perfectly," she claimed. It was then that I saw more human artwork within the yew. "It's amazing."

"I count twenty faces in total," Becca reported. "That one looks like Mister Castelan. You remember, Hugo. You took his drama class, right?"

"Uh, yeah," I said, at a loss for words. She was right. His visage looked older than I recalled, with a frightened expression. It was a wooden likeness of Castelan. I was convinced that there were no more familiar forms when my eyes caught an image.

Three foot out from a high cluster of thick branches was a wooden man's upper torso. Arms outstretched and from what could be interpreted as wrists sprouted leaf bearing limbs. Above the neck, a head was positioned against an upper branch. I recognized that face. It belonged to my brother Dalton's oldest friend, Terry Drew.

"Do you know any of the others," asked Becca.

"Nope," I insisted.

I needed more information before talking to Dalton. It just seemed prudent to tell him before announcing it to the rest of the town.

"We should be getting back," insisted Becca.

"You start," said Wilona. "I'll catch up in a minute."

"Okay." Becca was skeptic. "Hugo, I'll you soon."

"Sure," I responded. "I'll give you my number and address."

"Not necessary." Her certainty was baffling. Did have my information or was she 'blowing me off'? Becca Webb stepped back up the makeshift stairs, leaving me with Wilona.

"Becca's a lovely girl," she claimed. Her hands

came from behind and down my chest. I was nervous again. "You like me better anyway. Right, Hugo?"

Convinced that I had a crush on Becca, my eyes turned to meet Wilona. Had I changed my mind? My lips parted and an agreement was about to emerge.

"This could be our private haven, baby," she interrupted. "Our special garden."

"Hugo?"

I turned to see December standing near the brook chasm. Over her right shoulder was an off-white purse with gold accents and red flower patterns. As soon as my sister's voice was heard, Wilona removed her soft finger.

"I'll see you later," the former cheerleader claimed. With a smile, she moved past my sister and up the stairs.

"That looked cozy," December remarked.

"She was a big tease in high school," I confessed. "She never touched me though."

"Well, it's good to see your social life is improving." Looking beyond some foliage, she shouted, "Come out!"

Zeke trudged from hiding. In a huge t-shirt and jeans, he stepped next to our sister. The pale eyes seemed to stare past as his mouth beamed.

"December," he said like a big child. "She, my sister."

"That's right, Zeke," she confirmed.

"What's he doing here?" I asked. "Aren't you afraid the law will see him?"

"I didn't have much of a choice," December explained. "Gypsy left him without warning, and I had to get here in a hurry."

"Why is that?" I questioned.

"I saw you at this people tree," she announced, pulling a four-inch diameter sphere from her purse. It was an amethyst geode she'd discovered at *the pits* behind our mother's house. December was able to see images from its sparkling purple surface. In mystic accounts, it's called *scrying*. "You have a stalker."

"Mrs. Kastleberg hasn't bothered me since this morning," I joked.

"You know what I meant. Whoever he is, I get a strong vibe." My expression was the same as people gave when I told them that I see ghosts. She responded, "He's got a twinge of vis around him, like the bogle. Remember?"

"Was I supposed to forget the scarecrow with the death touch? You're saying the wobble headed stalker is a monstrum?"

"I'm still new to this but I believe so." December returned the stone to her bag. "He may have been brought here."

"From where?" I asked.

From the purse came a crossword puzzle magazine and a folded piece of paper. Most would have found her sudden need to show off the little book as odd. Not me. Even before she inserted the paper into the magazine, I knew what she was doing. The soft pages morphed into a larger hardbound volume.

"You didn't pull *Tools for Practical Witchcraft* from that geode," I stated. "How'd you get it."

"Stopped by your apartment," she admitted. "There were guests, so I helped myself. Figured you'd want to use it."

"Guests at my crib? Are they drinking? It's not even noon yet!" I complained. "It's bad enough that they show up at all hours of the night. Now they're breaking in?"

"No, I think your girlfriend opened up."

"My girlfriend?" I realized what she was alluding to. "Colleen. She must have made a key behind my back. What did she want?"

"She was waiting for you," my sister said as I

took the book.

Flipping to the glossary, I said, "I suppose you've already been snooping in here."

"I just looked up scrying," she confessed. "It said that only two types of people can naturally do that with precious stones."

"I know; a witch or a sorcerer."

"Sorceress," she corrected. "With the trouble you've had with the author, I have to believe that being a witch isn't the positive experience Wiccans report. How bad is being a sorceress?"

"That's the trouble, sis," I said. "The contents change. I've tried looking up *sorceress* but haven't had any luck."

"I couldn't find anything relating to your stranger either," she claimed.

"Stranger," Zeke said.

"Yes, Zeke," I replied. "The entry for the yew tree is basically what you'd expect. Don't eat the leaves because of toxicity. Oh. Then there's this sentence at the end. *The yew is the traditional roost of the harpia.* What's that supposed to mean?"

"The yew," repeated Zeke.

The sound of moving vegetation caused heads to turn. We saw that the stranger had returned.

"I don't get it. He's odd but not monstrum

odd. He is probably spying though," I admitted. "I can only think of one person who'd want me watched and has the power to summon monstrum."

"Monstrum," stated Zeke then marched off toward the stranger.

"No, Zeke," December yelled as she ran after him.

"There's not enough to look this guy up," I told myself.

"Hugo." The new voice was familiar but had a subtle distortion. It sounded like talking into a pipe. My eyes followed my name until they stopped below the wooden image of Terry Drew. Floating slightly above the earth was a translucent blue apparition. It was Terry. "Help us, Hugo."

Once I'd heard the plea, the blue form vanished.

Chapter Three: Exchanging Info

I leaned the bicycle to dismount. The arboretum stroll, and the twenty-minute ride with a bent peddle, had reduced my hamstrings to tight masses of pain. Regardless, clutching the frame's top tube, I placed the bike against my deltoid and carried it in and up the apartment building stairwell. My strength *edge* may have failed but the rest of me had to carry on.

The door to apartment B was slightly ajar. With the tip of a foot, the entrance was nudged enough to allow me and the ten speed inside. Clicking the kickstand in place, the bike was left between the restroom door and refrigerator.

Two unknown women sat in chairs around my folding table. In the third chair was the woman that had been sleeping on my bedroom floor earlier. She was on Bentley Adcock's lap, looking at the three cards in her hand. The whole group was in on the game. There were two decks, one for discards, on the grey surface, along with a couple 40-ounce beer bottles and my last package of crackers.

"What's up, Hugo," greeted the girl on Bent's lap. She introduced herself, Tess Lauren, as well as the other two. My preoccupied mind forgot her friends as soon as the names were spoken.

"Nothing personal, guys," I explained, looking at the carpet. "I've had very little sleep and still have to work tonight."

"No prob, HG," Bent responded. "We'll keep the noise down."

"I was actually hoping to have the place to myself," I replied. The group looked disappointed yet, a few seconds later, Bent's demeaner changed.

"Oh. I get it," he decided, setting his cards down. "Sure thing, man. Alright, let's leave Hugo and his girl alone."

"My girl?" I considered his words then realized he was talking about Colleen Kastleberg. I'd almost forgotten about her. "Oh. Where is she?"

"She's in the bedroom," said Bent as the group made their way down to ground level. I closed the door. I didn't hear movement from the front of the apartment. This drove me to urgently wanting a look at the *Harpia* in Switch's book (technically it's a love letter from Heart to me). Hoping not to be disturbed, I locked myself in the restroom.

"The harpia must be conjured from an alternate reality," I understood from the page. "What's the difference between alternate realities and dimensions? Anyway, once here, it transforms an indigenous species of tree into *Taxus Baccata*, a yew tree? It gets worse. It must hunt, kill, and eat a female victim to keep from being torn apart by our reality. Successful, the harpia assumes the initial victim's form, personality, etc. whenever it desires. The disguise is a crucial part of its hunting strategy."

Done reading, I placed the book in the cabinet beneath the sink. Stepping out and around the bike, the entry wouldn't leave my thoughts.

After the initial kill, the book claimed that a harpia must perch on the yew in its avian form. This must be done no less than two hours a night. Next to the synopsis was the drawing of a vulture body with huge metallic-looking talons. Beneath its feathered chest were human breasts and, from neck up, the harpia looked like a homo sapien.

My feet stopped at the closed bedroom door. Perhaps because it would otherwise be torn from reality, but the bird form of the harpia had to perch on the yew for no less than an hour in the evening. The trouble was that it couldn't perform that act until it added life to the plant when the sun was up.

"The carvings aren't art. They're victims," I responded, suspicious.

Their bodies looked like they'd been converted to tree fiber. The images showed no signs of breathing. Terry Drew was the final clue. He might have gone to the tree with a pumping heart but, when I arrived, he was a ghost. "No. They're dead. There might be a spell to reverse the damage but I'm doubtful."

Another issue I had when I started the article: Was the trench coat stalker the harpia? That question had a straightforward answer. No.

The harpia's first victim had to be a woman. The bumbling stranger was not a woman.
On that subject, there was nothing in the article about the gender of the tree sacrifice. I couldn't be certain, but I thought I'd seen the faces of women on that tree. I guess they could have been dudes with lady characteristics.

"Wake up," I shouted after entering the room. Colleen Kastleberg was fully clothed, laying on the waterbed. Her eyes opened as I raised my voice. "You need to go!"

An angry storm moved across her pale face then, as quickly as it had come, facial muscles softened. Her hands went to my waist, and she gave a gentle tug. Her intent was to bring me onto the free flow mattress but found resistance. Once the effort was found to be futile, Colleen used me to pull herself to a standing position.

"I know I shouldn't have come but I've missed you," she claimed with tears in her eyes.

I'd been through a multitude of incidents where she verbally destroyed my self-worth. Unable to take more, my mind turned cold. My new goal was to get away from her. The trouble was my emotions. They could never harden enough to keep Colleen from manipulating me.

She'd cry and act the part of the victim. My iron will would evaporate every time.

"Get out," I repeated, close to giving in again.

"Hello?" It was Wilona's voice coming from the apartment door. I had closed but not locked the entrance. Why would I when there was still someone of need of eviction? "Hugo, are you around?"

"In the bedroom," I responded.

Colleen's storm returned. I would have grinned but was still upset that she'd invited herself into my apartment.

"Oh, you have company," Wilona responded with a brief look of disappointment. "I can come back another time."

A second before, I saw a spark of enthusiasm on her chestnut countenance. Did she think I was alone? I considered the outcome of that scenario. My emotions pulled between desire for Willo and arousal verses bitterness toward Colleen. Before the former cheerleader entered, I was tempted to rip my clothes off and submit to Mrs. Kastleberg's mind screwing.

Once Willo stepped to the foot of the waterbed, I wished Colleen had *gone to play in traffic.* Even so, as much fun as time with the former schoolmate sounded, I needed rest. I was scheduled to work that evening.

"Hi, I'm Wilona but you can call me Willo," she said, holding out a slightly bent wrist. Colleen took it in both hands as though cherishing a special gift.

"I'm Colleen." she responded.

Being in my early twenties, I fantasized a lot. Even so, I could almost breath the unspoken sensation that passed between the women. As soon as Wilona made eye contact, Colleen looked like she'd spent the day lounging at the beach. We, men, are typically awful at romantic queues so I decided that I was misreading the situation.

"She was just leaving," I proclaimed.

Mrs. Kastleberg looked at me for a moment, surprised, then back at Wilona. Colleen opened her mouth, but nothing was uttered.

"Chill, playa. Colleen and I can exchange information and talk another time. Girl talk, you know," Wilona said, then glance at me. "She'll be out of your hair in a jiffy."

"I'd like that," Kastleberg replied and the two walked into the front room. I couldn't get inappropriate images off my male brain while I waited.

"I get the impression that your breakup wasn't mutual," Wilona stated. Colleen had left.

"Depends on what phase of the moon you catch her in," I joked.

Seeing Willo's inquisitive reaction, I tried to elaborate.

"Colleen messed with my head to the point that I can't stand the sight of her," I claimed. The truth was far more complicated. While a part of me would be ecstatic if she were maimed by a moving vehicle, another desired nothing less than to touch, kiss, or embrace the Colleen I once found so adorable. "She did a real number on me and it's difficult."

"But you're ready to move on," she asked.

"I moved on. There was a woman, after Colleen, but she strung me and another guy along. That doesn't mean I want Colleen back! She screws with my head."

"I guess its good that I don't swing that way," she claimed, touching my chest. "She just looked like a girl in need of a shoulder. I hope you don't mind."

Her warm grin told me that her words were beyond scrutiny. As our lips aligned, I wanted to believe her. All the while, my single most reliable *edge* interpreted her differently. Inching toward one another, my moment with Willo was shattered by knocking. It was the apartment entrance.

"Fob! She's back," I complained.

"I'll have a talk with her, baby," Wilona volunteered.

"No," I replied, irritated with the whole Colleen situation. "Wait here. I'll take care of it. She won't be back."

I marched from the room, around the couch made from old mattresses and into the next room. Walking between the card table and the dresser used for my hotplate, I stepped to the door. Grabbing the handle, I turned and pulled.

"What!" I barked.

"Gees, bro," Dalton responded, stepping forward. Vince Sorum Jr. accompanied him. "That's no way to answer a door."

"Thought it was the Kastleberg woman, huh," CIA Vince suggested. "We saw her walking to her car."

"I'm kind of preoccupied right now. Tell me what you want and get out," I insisted.

"You haven't seen me in over six months, blood," said Dalton. He was wearing an expensive blue suit with lighter colored tie. A state representative pin was attached to the lapel. "That's some way to treat your kin?"

"Don't take it personal, Dalton," expressed Vince, wearing the same outfit as earlier that morning. There was a manila folder tucked under his arm. "Your brother gets like this when there are women involved. My guess is that he still has one up here."

Dalton looked toward the front room. I followed his gaze to find Wilona walking toward us. My brother held his hand out to give his typical political greeting. This usually included a laser focused eye contact. On this occasion, however, he turned back toward me.

"Lovely girl," he said as she shook Vince's hand. The CIA operative introduced himself as my landlord, Vito. She accepted the deception, said her goodbyes, and left.

"That girl's all wrong," the two men said in unison. Before I could respond, Vince spoke again. "December contacted Dalton, here. He got in touch with Cadadrius which sent me."

"About Willo?"

"Willo, is it?" Dalton questioned. "You've got enough problems right now. Do yourself a favor and stay away from…Wilona."

"What does that mean?"

"If you were any other guy in this situation, Hugo," began Vince. "I'd tell you that girl is way out of your league. There's not a blemish or flaw to be seen. She dresses intentionally plain, showing every healthy body curve, and applies the most minimal of makeup. That girl knows exactly what men see when they check her out. Wilona wants something from you, kid, but it sure isn't the insecure, minimum wage earner I know."

"You're just full of confidence boosters. Aren't you, CIA Vince?"

"He's being blunt but it's true, bro," chimed in Dalton. "Besides, I'm not here to slam your taste in women. Vince and I want to talk about the guy that's been following you."

"The dude with the neck disorder?" I inquired. "He might have had harmful intent but, after Zeke ran off, I got concerned. Is the poor guy alright?"

"He didn't have a neck disorder," Vince claimed. "You have to have a…he isn't human."

"Oh, wait. I know," I guessed. "He's a she and she's a harpia right?"

"No idea what that is but you really are bad

with women, aren't you?" judged Dalton. "No. This thing is male, but it isn't from around here."

"Cadadrius has it in custody, but it isn't talking. We don't even know if it speaks a discernible language," Vince admitted, handing over a photo from his folder.

The image was of a decapitated body strapped to a physician's table. Portions, like the golden toned limbs and genitalia appeared human. I noticed a lengthy mark crossing the center of the sternum region and one on each shoulder. The assumption was that the stranger had sustained injuries when it encountered Zeke.

"The whole neck is gone but there's no sign of a wound. Was he killed with a laser?"

"It's not dead, bro," stated Dalton, motioning toward Vince.

Another photo came from the folder and into my hand. This picture was similar except the body's chest wound was open, exposing oversized human teeth. Also, the slits on its shoulder sockets were open. Each revealed an eyeball, glaring at the photographer.

"What is it?" I asked, handing back the prints.

"We don't know. One thing is certain. The head, that Zeke knocked off, was no more real than anything shown at a wax museum," said Vince. "That brings us back to you."

"Your book," Dalton stated. "We thought maybe you could look this thing up."

"I can try but it helps if you already know the name of the species," I explained. Stepping around Vince, I entered the restroom. Pulling out *Practical Tools for Witchcraft* from beneath the sink, I returned to the other room. "It doesn't always have what's needed at the time you're looking for it."

"We'll take our chances," Vince decided, taking the book. After looking through the glossary, he flipped through the whole volume before returning it. "There's nothing new."

"You had to have missed something," decided Dalton. "That book's huge."

"It repeats entries," assured the agent. "The Vilkaci article, for example, shows up at least three times."

"Strange," I stated then flipped back to the glossary. "I've had trouble with this book but nothing like what you described. Here's an entry for the *headless horseman*."

"A tall tale," claimed Dalton as I flipped to

the page.

"According to this, you're right," I stated. "See *Ewai <Ee-Way>*."

I flipped to the new reference page to find a sketch matching the features in the photos. I read the entry aloud.

Chapter Four: Fire or Sphere

Ewai <pronounced Ee-Way> comes from the species *Ewaipanoma*, which were first discovered on the banks of the Caura River (Venezuela) during the start of the 1600s. The word means *Headless One*. It is said that a dimensional hole formed between Earth and a geographic location on the planet Acephalus, in the Tau Ceti system (a yellow dwarf star and part of the constellation of Cetus the sea monster) some twelve light years distant. Within decades, the hole was distorted (erased) by a combination of global and climate shifts and alterations within the cosmic conduit. Like most monstrum, the only method for bringing one of these alien creatures to Earth, at present, is through conjuring.

The ewai female is not mentioned in historical references, but the males tend to have tan complexions and muscular bodies. Most ewai stand about five'2" (6'0" with disguise). Apart from a neck and head, much of their characteristics resemble Earth people. Differences include an eye located on each upper pectoral muscle. A long mouth stretching across…

"Looks like the rest is stuff we already know. Basically, the captured wobble-head is an ewai."

With my head downcast, I closed the book. "I'm sorry about Terry."

"Vince showed me a Tokeca Journal and Maashkinooze Trading Post article about the weird tree," explained Dalton. "As far as we know, the image is someone's idea of art. Terry's fine."

"I'm sorry," I said, flipping to the *Harpia* entry. "I don't think so."

"Fobbing bird-lady!" Dalton shouted after reading. He slumped onto a folding chair placing both hands over his eyes. Looking up again, he claimed, "I meant to drop by and talk to him, maybe mend things between us. The trouble was publicity from associating with dealers and addicts if the media discovered my visit. He was my best friend. I didn't even get to introduce him to Aggie. What about Sky, his girlfriend? Was she on the tree?"

"No, I don't think so," I said, sitting at another chair. "Two different monstrum, that can't be a coincidence. This has to be Switch's doing."

"We have to find this Harpy," Dalton announced, getting back to his feet. "Nico and I are expected in Cedar Rapids later today. You'll have to do the groundwork. Vince, can you help him?"

"Harpia, not harpy, and it shouldn't be tough," Sorum responded. "We'll stake out the tree. Whatever her human guise, this thing will have to return with a victim before the sun goes down."

"I have to get to sleep," I told them.

"You can't do this for me?" questioned my brother, with the apartment door open. "He was my best friend, Hugo."

"He'll do it," Vince said after a period of silence. I felt horrible suggesting that sleep was more important to me than finding the monstrum that killed Terry Drew. I couldn't look my brother in the eye. "I'm counting on you, bro."

Vince planned to have Dalton picked up. When he returned to my apartment, I was jotting down notes. At the top of the page was written 'Notes for *Profanus Files*.

"Let's get going," Vince suggested. "We'll want to get there before her. Besides, I figure we better stop off for snacks and drinks. The sun goes down in less than six and a half hours, but it still might be a long wait."

"Fobbing family," I said, dropping my pen into the notebook. "Let me call work. Obviously, I'll be in no shape to go in tonight."

"Yeah, Erotic Kingdom will be hard pressed

to sell all those adult toys without your help," Vince smirked.

"It's a job," I argued. "Some of us don't get paid by the government to do…whatever it is you do."

"I'm thankful for that," Vince admitted, from outside the apartment door. I made the call and was treated to guilt. Inevitably, I hung up. Before locking the door, I grabbed the notebook and the letter from the crossword magazine.

In front of the building, Vince got into an '89 Chevy Astro CL with government license plates. By the time I'd gotten in the passenger side and fastened my belt, it dawned on me that Vince was staring out the rearview mirror. The van was running but we weren't moving.

I asked, "What's up?"

"Not much," he replied. "All set?"

I nodded. To my surprise, after engaging Reverse, he rushed the white vehicle entirely too fast. I felt the bumper make contact then Vince shifted the stick behind the steering wheel to Park and unbuckled his safety strap. His door was left wide open as he walked to the rear.

More noise was followed by the double rear doors swinging out, pouring sunlight over my perception. He grunted as he pushed a load into the cargo area. Adjusting my eyes, I heard raw clicking. I was sure it was handcuffs, but the sound came in multiple patterns.

Once Vince was back in the driver's seat and we were moving up Iowa Avenue, I inquired, "What was that?"

"Your stalker wasn't alone," he smiled.

"Colleen?" I blurted.

"No, Hugo," he replied, disappointed. "The ewai. Whoever sent him, brought a backup."

"Are you saying you hit one in the street and put him in the back of the van?" I considered what that must have looked like from a street view. "It's daylight. Weren't you afraid someone would notice?"

"Doing the unusual tends to get less attention than ordinary behavior," Vince claimed.

As we pulled into a DunRight Fast-and-Gas convenient store, I responded, "Uh, huh. Where'd you learn that bit of wisdom, CIA ethics class?"

The agent smirked while removing a couple of twenty-dollar bills from his pants. Handing them over, he listed off his shopping list and offered to buy my snacks too.

At the entrance to the store, I looked back.

Vince walked around the front of the vehicle and back along the passenger side. I presumed he was accessing the cargo area via the sliding door. My suspicion was later confirmed when I saw the rifle between the front seats.

Inside the store, my first area of interest was the front shelves where I found chips, jerky, snack cakes, and two Berritopia Slushburgs. By the end of the isle, my hands were holding a load of junk food and ice drinks against a damp, chilled belly. I passed a section of beverage coolers then veered into the center grocery isle. Looking up, a set of pink lips smiled my way.

"Becca?"

"I figured you'd be asleep by now," Becca Webb commented. "Don't you work nights?"

"Yeah. I'm doing a favor for a family member," I explained.

"Not December, I suppose," she said. "She was just in here buying snacks. There was a big guy in the car with her. From the looks of your choices, she eats a lot healthier than you."

"Some of this is for the driver," I explained. "He's buying. You know how that works."

"Sure. Anyway, I was telling December about the yew tree, but she said that she's already been there. Funny thing. She was going back. It didn't seem that popular when me, you, and Willo went," she stated. "By the way, have you seen her?"

"Wilona? I, uh, saw her go past the hotel after I got home." How was I supposed to tell her that her friend came straight to my crib, virtually undressing me with her beautiful eyes. "I thought she had an appointment with you."

"She bailed," Becca complained. "I was so upset that I cancelled both appointments."

"Why. My mom claims that pedicures are relaxing. It sounds like what you need." As we talked, I thought about the area around our earlier visit. That yew tree had made both local papers over the last few days. In our town, publicity was reason enough for popularity seekers to show up in droves. Everyone in a thirty-mile radius should have been rushing to be the one to claim they'd seen it. No, the lack of spectators was unusual even that early in the morning.

By the time we reached the register, Becca had decided to reschedule her appointment. After paying, I commended her decision and took the bag of munchies to the van. Seeing the gun tucked between bucket seats, I commented, "A gun, huh."

Shooting the harpia from a safe distance made

sense. Why let it tear either of us apart or allow ourselves to be convinced to merge with that tree. Being in the CIA, I didn't doubt Vince was a crack shot. I had watched spy movies most of my childhood. It was a given, realistic or not, that all government agents were badass super spies.

No. My worry was over Switch's book. It hadn't expressly outlined a method for eliminating the harpia. It wasn't uncommon to find an entry like it but, like an ingredient in a recipe, I felt more confident when it listed exactly how to take a monstrum down. Would a high-powered rifle do the trick?

At around one in the afternoon, the white van pulled into the arboretum parking area. Vince grabbed the gun and a case of extra equipment. Heart's letter went in my pocket before getting out of my seat. With my notebook in the snack bag, a grabbed it and the drinks.

We were off the paved path and well along the dirt trail by the time we encountered December and Zeke. Ten feet ahead, they were both on the ground. December sat in the grass, holding her stomach while the sound of vomiting coming from my brother.

"Something's wrong. Zeke's been through

every physical torment imaginable. He's beyond showing sickness," I said. "And she's sick at the same time?"

"Food poisoning," Vince suggested, taking a sip from his drink. "We should keep moving."

A few feet closer and Sorum set down his stuff. I was about to ask if he was alright when he got on his knees to harf.

"This isn't right," I said, feeling my insides turn to jelly. I stepped back as the urge to hurl started. No sooner had I retreated then the ill sensation vanished. I went to Vince and pulled him out. "It's some sort of barrier. That's how the harpia keeps intruders from viewing her human sacrifice."

"Where was it before?" Vince asked, feeling better.

"It must only show up when the harpia has someone near the tree."

As I spoke, the agent ran in for his stuff and back out again.

"Sorry, kid, but it's going to be up to you to reach the tree," he declared, then took another sip of his drink. "I know how awful you'll feel if that thing gets another victim."

"Where are you going?" I asked as he stepped

off the path. "Don't you care?"

"If she gets away, it's just a mission. This is your town," he confessed. "I'm taking a walk through the woods to see if I can get a decent vantage point from this side of the barrier. If I fail, I'll try again tonight while she's in her feathered form."

His cold logic aggravated me but, from his perspective, it made sense. Frowning, I watched Vince fade into the wilderness. What actions did I have left? I wasn't going to intentionally turn my back on the harpia's intended prey. Picking up my stuff, I stepped forward.

I'd only been in the sick zone less than a minute when I dropped my ice drink. It looked awful and my stomach churned. December was within hands reach when I turned to vomit. Coincidently, the barf went all over the discarded plastic Slushburg cup.

"Go back," I told December. "You'll feel fine if you leave."

"My head feels like it's being bombarded with fire," she complained. I nodded, feeling the same.

"It's magic," I explained as she crawled to safety. Turning toward Zeke, cramps tightened within my abdomen. I fell. "I can't reach Zeke."

December calmly watched my struggle. She'd made it from the infected area, contemplating her next move. I grabbed at my grocery sack, trying to stand at the same time. Dizzy, I had trouble using my eyes.

"I see two women gawking at that horrible tree. One is Carver's mother, the other is Becca's friend," December explained, staring into her amethyst sphere. She looked up and contemplated. "If a spell is holding us back than there must be a counter; a charm or amulet."

"No feel good," complained Zeke. "Tummy rot!"

"Colleen and Willo? It all makes sense now," I mumbled as my frame felt like vibrating rubber. Thoughts for the women voided December's analysis of the ill barrier. "Wilona never liked me in school but has been trying to get me alone this whole time. Poor Colleen, Willo's going to kill her!"

I wobbled to my feet with the bag dangling from one fist. I stepped to Zeke.

"Go back!" I said, walking forward. My whole body felt like it might erupt into a flaming mass of intestinal fluid. I couldn't see my brother anymore. I could barely make out the trees. Not more than twenty feet beyond the last place I'd seen my brother, the pain became so great that I collapsed onto the path.

With nothing more to unload, my body went into crouch mode and convulsed. The dry heaves lasted some exceptionally long minutes. My palms felt around in the soil as I considered pushing myself upward. I imagined standing when my fingers touched a smooth object. With all the agony, the simple ball shaped object felt good. Looking closely, it turned out to be December's geode

"Where are you?" I called. How had it gotten there? Did I steal it? I couldn't imagine doing that to her. Squinting in the direction I'd last seen her, everything was a blur. "They left me. Good. At least they're safe."

"You will be safe as well, dear boy," stated Garius DeMorney. I looked around but didn't see him. The voice must have been part of a delusion brought on by anguish. Confirming my hypothesis, the stone had consumed my hand and lower arm. I tried to scream but my throat was arid. The heaving started again as the globe absorbed the rest of me and spit me back together. My body was intact in a familiar janitor closet

"The high school," I realized. The suffering was gone though it was a tight fit with December, giant-like Zeke, and a bunch of cleaning supplies. I heard the crinkling of the shopping bag while observing the ghostly image of Garius. "You."

"We have had our differences, Auger Grazer, yet I couldn't stand by and allow you to be killed," he stated. "Clearly there will be no talking you out of this action. With that in mind, I am using my limited power to push the geode."

"Who asked you?" I barked.

"I wasn't going to argue. My brain was on fire," admitted December. "Where are you taking my stone?"

"Head better," said Zeke with a slight squeal at the end of the statement.

"To the yew tree, Lady December," Garius replied.

Chapter Five: Barbra

The latex expression remained neutral while rocking through the wilderness. Beyond white doll hair and cheap sunglasses, its features were identical to those worn by the captured ewai. The disguise was held on top of the monstrum by a white shirt.

Over it was a blue tracksuit with three stripes running the length of both arms. The jacket had been modified with plastic discs, of the same shade, sewn into the shoulders. Except from long distances, the ewai's huge eyes were still visible. Moving by a group of slender trees, a bulge showed across the rear of the outfit.

Past yellow leafed Maples, the wanderer discovered a feminine figure. Raven hair flowed over black silk-cotton fabric. The form fitted outfit covered her arms with red curved lines. The same design ran vertically from band collar to waist, pausing three inches, then more pronounced horizontal lines arched along the hips. Capris leggings continued the pattern.

Pale feet pressed into a section of wooden flooring, covered by her buttocks and October weeds. Three digits of each hand were positioned against her temples. A fireplace stood to the left of the path.

The ewai understood that the mishmash of indoor furnishings and wilderness was purely psychological. The smooth skinned woman was not at the arboretum nor was he in the cupola of the Maashkinooze Octagon Lodge.

"Your report, familiar," she ordered with closed eyes. The Argentinian blue shoulder orbs of the ewai focused, cross-eyed, on the speaker.

"The she-bird is preparing another sacrifice,

Mistress. Your foe, Grazer, was in the vicinity but now eludes me. I believe the bitter repellent of your harpia has either brought about the demise of he and his ilk or they've fled," he divulged. His voice was normally high pitched and gravelly. Speaking through the tracksuit added a muffled quality. "Before this audience, I was tracking the Cadadrius operative. He was carrying an M82 rifle."

"Mr. Sorum intends to hunt my pet," she concluded. "That can't happen. Lose the façade, familiar. Track and eliminate Vince Sorum Jr. Report back when you've finished."

From the ewai perspective, the great witch evaporated, along with all objects usually foreign to the outdoors. The familiar unzipped and removed the jacket, followed by the undershirt. The fake head fell to the ground with the discarded apparel. Unfastening the sling between left collar bone and right waist side, the monstrum accessed a leather tube.

His chest opened enough for an enormous tongue to reveal itself. It licked the edges of the mouth then returned to the body's interior.

A handful of pieces were taken from the tube. The ends of two fiberglass-aluminum pieces were clicked together then a central handle was cranked until the portable bow was taut. Once the quiver had been snapped to his back, the ewai grabbed for an arrow. Once placed against one of the strings, the monstrum charged after his prey.

Rising, Mistress Switch exposed dark blue eyes. The mental link with the arboretum monstrum had faded, leaving an octagonal room with four hearths.

"Empusa Brynhild," the witch called then snapped her fingers. Brynhild Aelfweard instantaneously appeared in the chamber. The subordinate performed a curtsey before addressing the great witch.

"Mistress, what is required of me?"

"Many of your sisters are assisting with our Penumbra project," Switch explained. "We have the Iraq agenda. Empusa Godleaf has assured that their president, Hussein, should be ready to attack neighboring Kuwait within months. As you are aware, the coven has been stoking fires within the U.S. government as well. Empusa Treasure believes that America will follow Saddam not long after his invasion. Another catalyst will be needed to guarantee a long-term commitment but, as soon as empusa Sibylla and Joan can be pulled from assignments in Russia and China, plans will commence."

"As you've often said, One-witch," Brynhild relayed. "Chaos and confusion; it's why witches were designed."

"On that note, I have summoned you to discuss a local matter," Switch announced then her expression hardened. "I went through a great deal of trouble conjuring my latest exotic pet."

"Yes, Mistress. The harpia."

"When I've sufficiently nurtured her, it is my goal to add to her numbers. I envision a kettle of these birds soaring between perches in a forest of macabre yew trees."

"It sounds glorious, Mistress."

"Yet the usual thorn in my side has stumbled into her feeding ground. This is where you come in," Switch announced. "Keep Hugo and his family from harming my pet. If my harpia can merge Mr. Grazer with the yew, so be it. Otherwise, do what it takes to allow my darling scavenger free reign."

"Mistress," Empusa Brynhild insisted. "Hugo

has, albeit haphazardly, been a challenge in the past and you, yourself, have expressed concern in regard to the sister."

"Yes. She has natural abilities, possibly beyond those within the coven," agreed Switch. "I, of course, am the exception."

A glint showed in Brynhild's eyes. Switch knew the look, a cross between greed and hunger. If the subordinate were a shark, she thought a trace of blood was in the water.

"Beyond the use of the aliens, ewai," pleaded the empusa. "I request special assistance."

Switch put the potential stench of treachery aside and considered the request. Looking around the room, her gaze stopped at a long-stemmed flower growing from a ceramic pot.

"I shall loan you my Heart," she claimed then turned to Brynhild's questioning grimace. "Your shoes."

The subordinate quickly removed a pair of white leather Keds. The great witch motioned toward the plant and the tennis shoes were dropped next to the ornate bowl.

"Dracula Simia," began Switch, followed by a

quick series of Latin sentences. Brynhild had lived an exceptionally long time yet still didn't have the skill to decipher the fast spoken incantation.

Switch went silent, grabbing the lowest part of the plant stem, then tugged it from the container. Dirt fell as the roots were moved upward then on top of Brynhild Aelfweard's favorite footwear.

"Heart!" commanded Hema Bridgette Switch.

The petals of the flower, which slightly resembled a face, turned toward Mistress Switch. They melted into the plant. The mass inflated until an actual head was observed. The tiny mouth screeched in pain as the stem formed thin appendages. Roots fused to create misshapen feet then the mass grew. It altered until a withered woman stood in the dirty tennis shoes.

"Yes, Heart. I have brought you back but not as an empusa," Switch stated while looking over the woman's haggard complexion. A familiar section of skin was missing from the side of her face. It was clearly visible through thin sporadic sections of hair. "You are simply a servant."

Heart rocked into a semi upright stance. Her mouth opened but only air escaped. Switch touched her creased forehead.

"Assist Empusa Brynhild. This assignment will decide if you are worth returning to the sisterhood or eternally removed from my sight," said the great witch.

Heart's skin had smoothed. She quickly appeared youthful, exposing a stern but gorgeous jawline. Her near-white hair had grown back to its long, feathered appearance.

"Follow the empusa but my will prevails," Switch declared, looking coldly into Heart's gold-green stare. "Do not disappoint me."

Snapping her fingers, Empusa Brynhild and the servant vanished. Still, a visual imprint of Heart Seacord's features lingered, taking the great witch to memories from February 2, 1567.

Sixteen-year-old Joan Waterhouse had lived among the coven of witches for about seven months. She'd witnessed the use of incantations, charms, even divination. Due to a limited understanding of the world, these things intrigued the girl. It didn't, however, alter her distain for a life of servitude amongst a band of meanspirited women.

That evening, Joan was brought to a round chamber. Eleven women, clad in black robes, stood against log walls. The one-witch, Dacian, was positioned a foot from three interlocking circles drawn in the center of the lengthy. Waterhouse was guided inside the markings, next to another girl.

"Barbra, hider is Joan," Mistress Dacian introduced, motioning to the other sixteen-year-old. "Neither hast met until anon because thou art candidates for one position. We hath furnished ample timeth to consider ye privilege. Tonight, one shall taketh her rightful place as thirteenth member."

Empusa Dionysia tossed a pair of daggers within the rings. Barbra snatched one, taking a stance where she could easily thrust at the other girl. Watchful of the blade wielder, Joan walked over and picked up the remaining weapon.

"Whichever performeth hider first ritual shall be mine own," Mistress Dacian explained.

Barbra crouched, ready to strike, until the details of the ritual were explained.

The candidates were momentarily relieved that they would not be fighting to the death. Disgust returned as a self-inflicted torture was described. Both must slice into the left festoon, just below the eye. This incision would move to the earlobe, along the jawbone then up along the corner of the child's mouth. The outlined area had to be filleted from the face. The winner would be disfigured while failure was punished by execution.

"Shalt it best Barbra or Joan?"

Two angry girls brought the daggers to their flesh. Tears of horror were expressed by one while the other showed resentful determination. The agony was excruciating but Joan used the sharp tip to create an outline. Every time the pain caused her to pause, she thought of Agnes and Wilmina Waterhouse. Either would have gratefully mutilated themselves to avoid death.

It took over three hours, but Joan completed the bloody act. Barbra, however, had only half the edges cut.

"Hider honor sacrifice," Joan stammered as she held the piece of flesh toward the mistress. "I offer to the great witch."

"Congratulations, zealous apprentice," proclaimed Mistress Dacian.

Joan's pain was interrupted by screaming. She turned to a terror-stricken Barbra. Seeing the bulge of her eyes, the apprentice looked at the spectators.

The coven had dropped their hoods, but their flesh no longer appeared smooth. Each of the wrinkled faced women had the same disfigurement Joan had done to herself.

Empusa Cristobel placed a wet cloth over the girl's wound as Dacian took the flesh from her hands. The damp concoction stung at first then Joan's pain decreased to a minor inconvenience. A loaf sized box was placed before the great witch. Within, Joan's fresh section of face was added to twelve decrepit pieces. Dacian resealed the box then Empusa Wulfhild took it from her sight.

"To beginneth thy next phase, Barbra shall instruct thee," claimed the great witch.

The girls were equally surprised by the statement. Without warning, Dacian grabbed Joan's arm and pulled her from the floor drawings. Passing, the one-witch handed Joan's dagger to Empusa Sorcha. Barbra tried to lift her weapon, but the other point had already penetrated her belly region. Convulsing, steel shifted inside her pancreas, exited then plunged back into another spot. The coven chanted in unison as Sorcha stabbed a total of thirteen times. The bloody dagger clanged onto the floor. Viewing the lifeless mass at her feet, a grin formed through splotches of red. Sorcha left the circle and joined the incantation. The coven's voices rose until it sounded like the wilderness was screaming Latin.

Chapter Six: Wood If She Could

A feeling of softness brushed across Vince Sorum Jr.'s ear. At first, he wondered if it were a boxelder or Asian beetle. That benign notion cracked like the impact of tree bark as the shaft struck.

"Turkey feathers," he bellowed. It had been the shaft's supple fletching his ear had experienced. Realization brought his knees down and his body to spin toward the arrow's source. A second projectile shot through air that had once contained his skull.

Unable to spot the culprit, his index finger jerked a shot at an upward angle. A hundred and fifty yards across the arboretum, the agent picked up movement.

Standing between a maple tree and a lilac bush was a bipedal creature in tracksuit sweats and athletic footwear. The head was missing, and teeth gritted from the chest. Resembling the sketch from Hugo's book, it was the first time Vince had seen an ewai without its disguise.

The Acephalus native had drawn back his

next arrow. Vince was amazed at the alien's ability to aim with eyes so far apart. Cautious of its stellar marksmanship, Vince chose to run behind a nearby tree over shooting back.

"Hey, fella," he called from cover. He could hear the ewai moving through grass. "Rambo wants his bow back."

"Whose Rambo?" replied the loud, rasping tone.

Vince brought the barrel out enough to pinpoint his target. A .50 caliber burst struck through a location an average human kept his or her heart. The bow shot spun into the foliage as the weapon fell from the ewai's grasp. The monstrum had experienced a traumatic internal explosion as the round tore out its rear side. Staggering backward, Vince expected it to fall over. He was disappointed to see it recover.

Rushing forward, the archer's hands reached out for the portable weapon. A trigger pull put a round through its left eye, forcing the monstrum to the ground. The big mouth groaned as the limb dangled from its side.

Vince ran toward his adversary as it attempted to get back on its feet. At thirty yards, the agent saw a shiny object in its hand.

"Knife," Sorum identified as the ewai raised its hand. The blade released smoothly from its fingers and spun with a straight trajectory. Vince dodged to the right, came from around a red bush then fired at the ewai. It fell back into the high grass then stopped moving.

When close enough, Sorum caught sight of haze filming over the alien's one intact eye.

"Fobbing thing had super monocular vision," Vince said. "It aimed like a machine! I sure hope his skill level isn't the average for ewai."

The agent walked for a while, getting sick then adjusting his trek to avoid the harpia defense. He never got a clear view of the area around the yew tree but thought he heard voices from a distance.

"I can't understand what they're saying," he mumbled, sitting next to a tree. Playing back events in his mind, one thought seemed the most important. "Grazer took all the snacks."

"I suppose it resembles a Scots pine," Colleen Kastleberg confessed. "Not that I know the difference between one pine tree and another."

"But you can see the designer's smooth carve marks," suggested Wilona Schuster as the women stared at the yew tree. "I told you it would be awesome. Only an artistic genius could create this intensity."

"I don't know about intensity, Willo," admitted Colleen. "I knew a woman from Cartagena that carved cranes from Holm Oak. I thought she was extremely skilled until today. Her work didn't compare to this detail."

"Want to touch it?" asked Wilona.

"I'm not sure. If you do, watch out for the needles. In the paper, they were warning against ingesting pieces of the plant. It's poisonous," said Colleen, pointing to sharp leaves growing in dual rows along each twig. "It might be nice to get a feel for what the artist was trying to express though."

"Why do you assume that nature isn't the artist. The yew isn't the only lovely thing out here. Beauty is everywhere," responded Wilona then touched Colleen's hand. A spectral image formed behind them. A brief instant went by, then, it dissipated. Garius had gone unseen because their focus was each other. "I even find beauty in people I've just met."

"Seeing you away from Hugo's place," said Colleen. "What a wonderful coincidence."

"I want to touch it," Wilona claimed, looking away from Kastleberg. "I know you're scared so we should do it together."

Colleen was about to say something when an object on the ground captured her interest. It was a shiny sphere. Reaching down, she snatched up the colorful geode and pitched it into the wilderness.

"What was that?" asked Wilona.

"Just a stone," Colleen claimed. "You're right. When we tell people we were here, they'll ask if we touched it."

"On the other hand," Wilona giggled. "You read that the yew was poisonous."

"Only if you eat it, silly," responded Kastleberg.

"Don't touch it, Colleen," I shouted.

With Garius' help, I'd come from the janitorial closet, through the rock, and into the arboretum. By the time I'd gotten my bearing, and found the right place, my face was already discolored from the harpia sickness. The next sentence burst out as a sour sensation took over. "She's tricking you!"

Near a thorny shrub, my knees buckled. The queasy sensation of the harpia defense brough forth a torrent of vomit.

"Hugo MacArthur Grazer," Colleen raged. "Haven't you ruined my life enough?"

"Oh, give the poor man a brake, Hun. I think

he's jealous," Willo declared. "Definitely green. Hugo? Did you have a little too much to drink today?"

"He'll ruin the entire day," Colleen stated. "We should leave."

"If you want to go then let's do it. I don't know everything that's gone on between the two of you, but you have to live your own life," advised Wilona. "Don't let Grazer, or any other guy, dictate what's best for you. Why not touch the tree? That'd show him, Colleen, then we'll leave him to blow chunks in the woods."

Colleen shook her head and smiled.

"You're so right, Willo," Colleen decided.

My eyes blurred as the pain in my head intensified. Stressed arms reached out to stop them, but my side fell against the earth. My vision made out twin blobs shifting toward an enormous brown glob. The last image was the yew tree.

Having rolled onto my spine, I watched as a single blob returned from the walk.

"She's better off now, Hugo," a voice declared as my physical agony subsided. When the enchantment ended, my sight cleared. The form, grinning down at me, had blond hair.

"Colleen," I sat up. "Thank heavens! You

didn't touch it."

"I did," she corrected, stepping back. "Baby, I can touch it anytime I choose. You don't own me!"

Staring from her irritated expression to the yew tree, I noticed something had grown from the trunk. It was a new carving. This one depicted a startled Wilona Shuster, looking over her shoulder.

"Kill that fob," demanded Terry Drew.

"He can't do that," replied Garius DeMorney. It was hard to ignore them since both ghosts hovered within my right arm's reach. "There must be a way to reverse this curse."

It's easier when others are around because they talk over the spooks. I just have to focus on the human conversation. No one else complains since I'm typically the only one who can see them. Relief came in the form of December and Zeke arriving.

"Leave him alone," December yelled at Colleen while stepping to my left side. "My brother wants nothing to do with you or your tree, Fob."

"I wasn't going to spoil your time with Hugo, dear. I was thinking I'd pay him a visit tomorrow." Colleen glared, then added, "You and I could have a little fun today though."

Zeke stepped in front of our sister, peering

down at Kastleberg.

"Buzz off!" His massive fist rose, shaking in front of her face. Colleen looked frightened until she noticed the surprised expression on both me and my sister's faces.

"Will," I tried to say but my pharynx was suddenly dry. "Wilona?"

"Yeah, Fob," Wilona said, walking from around the yew. There was another woman at her side. "I'm the only black girl out here and the hottest."

She giggled. I kept moving my focus from her, the wooden duplicate, and back again. While mentally trying to cipher that mystery, Wilona's companion walked up and wrapped her arms around my neck.

"Who are…"

"I've missed you so much, Hugo," she claimed. Gently pushing her to the extent of my arms, gold-green flex and limbal rings stared with an expectation. The needy manner her eyes fixated forced me to examine other features. She had the same lengthy white hair with the 80's feather style, a sensual rectangular jaw, and pleasant smile. Even minus the overabundance of makeup, she still looked like a twenty-five-year-old. It'd been four and a half years since the night they'd last seen each other.

"How is this possible?"

"Auger Grazer," Garius announced. "I believe Agent Sorum is standing behind those trees."

Twenty yards further along the trail, I spotted the agent. For an instance, his index finger was against his lips. Once he'd beckoned me to keep his location a secret, Vince dropped behind a yellow sumac.

"I see you still have those earrings," I said, rolling my eyes.

"Peridot," she admitted. "I almost lost them, if you remember."

"All this reminiscing over jewelry has been great but I'm bored," claimed Wilona. "Besides, Colleen wants to leave."

"Uh, yes," Kastleberg agreed. "I have my own life to live, Hugo."

"Sure," was my response plus a brief sideways glance. I had no idea what she was getting at and didn't want to translate the deeper implication. "Understood."

"Will. She's my ride too," Heart Seacord claimed.

"I didn't see you arrive with them," I puzzled.

She made an equally vague explanation before departing. Everyone else was silent until the three were well out of sight.

"I don't know what's going on, Hugo," December announced. "But I'm beginning to get onboard with Gypsie's distrust of your ex-girlfriend."

"That wasn't Colleen Kastleberg," Vince claimed as he approached. "She and the other woman weren't here before."

"What does that mean," December asked.

"It means that I've been standing over there," the agent pointed. "Long enough to see Mrs. Kastleberg's friends appear out of thin air. I've never seen the woman hugging Hugo but the other."

"Wasn't Wilona," I interrupted. "There was something about her, I can't place. She had an aura of cruelty about her, but it was different than Willo's. There was no desire to impress the crowd with her provoking skills. She's normally a master at teasing. It's hard to explain but her behavior didn't have the usual emotional sting. It wasn't her."

"Then she's the woman in the tree," December pointed to the yew image. "It also means that your other friend and Cooky Colleen are in trouble."

"That's just wrong," Terry Drew said but his words were lost on half the gathering.

"Friend might be a bit strong," I confessed. "Heart's a conundrum but I'm almost positive she used to work for bad people. That has to still be the case if she's with fake Wilona and Colleen."

"Do we know Mrs. Kastleberg is the genuine article?" questioned Vince.

"I saw two people walk to the tree and only one came back," I confessed. "Does that mean the survivor is this harpia?"

"Vince. How did you get over there in the first place?" questioned December. "You would have been stopped by illness."

"I think this filtered out the symptoms," Sorum announced, flipping a coin in the air. Landing in his hand, we saw that it was copper with the outer rim and interior details made from gold. Three interconnecting rings were etched on the surface.

"Magic circles," December announced. "That looks a lot like the talisman my sister told me about."

"Yeah. It belonged to Empusa Treasure," I confessed. "The symbol with a triangle top and sideways 'H' shaped lower is identical but the other rings have different symbols."

"I think it was given to an ewai so it could roam freely and pick off anyone that might be a threat to the harpia."

"E-way? Harpies?" my sister questioned. "Anyone want to tell me what's going on."

"Your brother can fill in the blanks when I'm gone," Vince replied. "Suffice it to say, the second ewai met its end. I found the coin amongst its archery gear. Now that I see everyone's in tiptop order, I need to go contact a cleanup crew. Cadadrius needs to erase a dead alien before prying eyes see it. We can't have people seeing invaders all over America. Someone might assume they're attacking folks."

Vince took a few steps then turned toward us.

"Okay, Grazers. Try to avoid anything out of the ordinary until I contact you again."

After he'd walked away, I began explaining about harpia and ewai to my siblings. We made our way out of the arboretum by the time the conversation was over. I collected my bike and went back to my apartment. With my shoes kicked in random spots, my destination was the bedroom. I was so worn out that I didn't bother to undress. My body flopped onto the waterbed and, by the time the waves settled, I was fast asleep.

Chapter Seven: Leaked Information

Joan Waterhouse stared at the dead body as the witches went from bellowing in rhythmic vocals to abrupt, implosive silence. Overcome by a sense of isolation, the teenager's arms shook.

An eternity passed in seconds before Mistress Dacian's footsteps broke the auditory void. She moved from the room's darker edges with a tome resting in one arm. Near Joan, her voice replaced the drumming of hard soles and the free hand made mystic gestures.

Waterhouse understood a smattering of Latin due to her time with the coven. In this case, one word stuck in her mind: *maleficia*. In her native language, it translated as *spelleth* or *enchantment*. A mild breeze drifted across her skin. One by one, the candle flames flickered then extinguished. This gave Joan concern for the result of whatever the great witch was bringing into the chamber. Dacian's stopped reading.

Before the last flame blew out, Joan got a glimpse of Empusa Sorcha's speckled expression. Her eyes gleamed like shimmering coal lodged in a face resembling granite.

From the somber atmosphere rose the repetitive shouting of a single word: *Leak*. Were the witches rooting for the maleficia's success? Was repeating that word just part of the ritual? Joan couldn't be certain.

In the deep black, her eyes caught a faint outline along the floor. The circles and symbols revealed themselves through inky blackness. The visual intensity increased until every marking glowed like ambers in a log fire.

From this new light source, the coven could see that Barbra's corpse was gone; not even a blood stain remained. Waterhouse, attracted by movement, discovered a murky outline within the maleficia rings. Frustratingly pacing, it had the bearing of a human male. As the candles were lit, she took in the stranger's features. His attire was sophisticated, almost aristocratic for the period. His body, conversely, was not the frame of a dandy. It was more on par with what the girl imagined the god Apollo might resemble. He was the most handsome man Joan had seen in her young life. His rugged jaw held a grin that seemed to have been designed especially for her. Her emotional defenses felt the stranger's gray eyes like a small blaze against an ice block.

"Who is this man?" Joan blurted, as the lights relit. Laughter passed between members then Mistress Dacian put her hand on Waterhouse's shoulder.

"This gent be no man, mine new empusa," she chuckled. "Prithee, Leak fugiens caput. Discover us thy true form."

At her request, most of Leak's frame dropped from his upper neck. Below was a series of gory entrails which followed its levitating head.

"This, mine lief, is an incidental daemon. Showeth her all, Master."

The handsome mouth opened and out flopped a massive tongue. Squirming, the dripping mass measured over two foot in length. Its girth was comparable to a cow's organ, far too wide to belong to a human. In addition, the daemon had two upper fangs which extended six inches from the gumline.

"He applies yond from which he speaks against dram girls liketh yourself and the late Barbra. His preferred meal wouldst be childing distaff and bawbling whelp yet a corpse may sufficeth, in a pinch."

"She was a tasty starteth," Leak admitted, rolling the gigantic tongue back into his face. "Begging your pardon. This new beldam looks even more scrumptious."

"Fugiens caput?" questioned Joan, stepping back.

"'Tis meaning is flying headeth," explained the great witch.

"Has yond gent come to consume me?"

"Nay," Dacian replied. "Thou art one of us anon. Never worry about thy safety. The daemon canst leaveth the maleficia rings lest permitted. The gent hath been invoked merely to usher thou between rituals. Master Leak, prithee presenteth thyself in a less hostile form."

In the blink of an eye, the daemon resembled the handsome figure of a man that had charmed young Joan. No longer comforted by the image, Joan stepped back a few feet. Finding the great witch absent, her face revolved until she spotted women. They were all leaving. Loneliness retook Joan as the final few were exiting. Dacian, the last, paused within the threshold.

"Keepeth with Leak till thy office is mere. The gent shalt proclaim when completeth. A warning, empusa. That daemon is powerful, deserving caution, yet never mistaketh courtesy for trustworthiness. Wherein thou hast finished, depart this chamber and presenteth thyself ere the coven."

The great witch closed the door, leaving Joan alone with Leak. She heard, from the other side, the thick wooden bolt placed in its cradles.

"What am I to tryeth?"

"A simple question, pathetic issue," claimed Leak. Eager to finish, Joan stepped forward. "What's thy nameth?"

"Joan. Joan Waterhouse," she answered.

"Oh, Joan Waterhouse. I know her as a victim. Primrose prey," declared the daemon. "Having not devoured thy bowels, I assumed you were another."

Joan's eyebrows hardened.

"Consume me? If ye be of limited value, vulgar beast, thee shalt beest dispatched."

"Thou frighten me not, whelp. Thee hath not the knowledge to sendeth me far afield," it claimed. "However. Belikes we couldst join to an arrangement?"

"Speak of the coven's requirement," Joan insisted.

"Absolutely," Leak agreed. "First, findeth an object."

"Object?"

"Exactness may not matter. A shoe shalt doth."

Joan removed her light leather footwear. Both were stitched along the rim with long points tied down to prevent tripping. Holding them out to the daemon, she inquired, "Now what?"

"Place thy poulaine upon a ringeth."

Joan brought one shoe forward but, as she began to bend down, stopped.

"Nay, goodyear. I surmise thy intent. If I obstruct the maleficia ring, thou art free to gnash mine flesh."

"Doth not hast to transpire. As I quoth, we may join in a desirable arrangement."

"Nay, fiend. Anon, wherefore we continue."

"Ye refrain from frightened Joan Waterhouse's language. Art thou not convinced of this identity? I distinguish flame within thy hearth, novice."

"Why am I hither?"

"Thou hast not concluded?"

"Nay. Suspicion tells me tis connected to a life of victimhood."

"Doth thou regard Empusa Preciosa's childhood nameth as Preciosa Constance McKain? Wast Empusa Sorcha aye Sorcha Jane Kaenylm?" There was a slight sound of reverence during the last sentence. "What of the most wondrous beldam herself? Was the lady aye Una Crina Dacian?"

"You hath declared each a liar before me?"

"Is Dacian the nameth of a human target, issue?"

"Of course not! She's the great witch and hath

faculties beyond mine comprehension."

"Not a hardy accomplishment, succulent. Doth thou imagineth any of the coven aye being berattled?"

"I supposeth, yet each is powerful anon."

"Assuredly. Nay longer sheep of the field, waiting to beest preyed upon."

"Thou imply each changed their title as to fulfill the empusa role."

"Like a bloody wound, each hath mended her designation to befit a durable condition."

"Ah. I am hitherto rest upon a name," Joan realized. "How? What shalt beest the alteration?"

"The empusa ritual stems from the first druid gatherings, 5,267 years since, in a lodging branded Gaul. Though many covens formed during yond time, thy dram band traceth its origins to the very Celts of 3700, before the time of his son. Those gents consulted stars, spake with woodland spirits, conspired with mine brethren. Never didst druids expect strangers to furnish their selfdom, Deary. Such a matter resides twixt the empusa and the ritual."

"I must inventeth mine own title? Brave," Joan determined. "Why, then, doth I require thou?"

"Oh, I beest of much help. Mineth vis assists thy

sisters' spellcasting. Thou require vis if thou art to become a significant coven member."

"Excellent. Thou aid in performing witchery," Joan surmised. "Understood. Anon how doth I nameth myself?"

"Oh, thou crave the rules," Leak considered. "Thou never imagineth inventing a name from sackcloth? Thou art clever."

"Silence, snarky pestilence! Sayeth the rules to me."

"Let us begin with the primrose, thy surname. Thou may deploy any fond family name or word, even combine text, yet must contain thy personal essence. This is mine station. As a judge, I decide if thy choice is acceptable. Shouldst I find the name displeasing, thou are required to begin anew."

Hours passed and Joan Waterhouse hadn't produced a single name which the daemon would back. She sat on the floor, tired and hungry.

"Skincarved," she blurted. It was a response to her current frustration. "That shall be mine surname."

"Do thou crave to be known as Lady Skincarved during the remainder of thy mortality? Thou are unaware yet some witches become so powerful that their existence is centuries long. The passing of a few hundred years may findeth Empusa Skincarved tiresome."

"May we forbear? I am famished."

"Excellent! This decision shouldst not beest taken lightly. Thou are transitioning thy entire state of affairs. Nay longer the victim but…"

"Transition," the girl considered. "I am switching from the life of victimhood to that of the dominant predator. Switching…hm? Mine surname henceforth shalt beest Switch!"

"There is certainty in thy youthful voice. Wherefore thy knowest it shalt not be vetoed, Ms. Casualty, akin to the previous idiotic names?"

"It is not akin to the others. I am positive yond surname hast no equal."

"Your sound beest confident. Methinks, it suits thee. Ay, dram empusa, we art closeth to revealing thy self. In bray out, cometh hither and grant me an embrace."

"Nay. Go onto the next nameth."

"You don't trusteth me?"

"As far as the ritual is involved, Master Leak. I'm certain thou must adhere to a process. The reason vexes me."

"It is simplistic. Thy leader hath high allies amongst Hell's legions. They expecteth participation in this ritual."

"So, if thou tricks a naive empusa into letting thou out of the circles? What happeneth then?"

"As much as I wouldst enjoy deception, the rules sayeth I must answer yond question earnest. Upon mine freedom, I couldst englut thou and the coven wouldst seeketh a replacement. Yond doth not hast to beest the issue. An arrangement may beest struck."

"The other names. How art each decided?"

"The mid traceth to the original Celts slaughtered by the Roman power. I shall bid forth a listeth of names. Picketh but one. Useth the name as it stands, addeth, or remove as long as the root name remaineth."

"Halt," Switch declared after the daemon spoke the thirty-eighth name. "That is the one!"

"Bricius is thy choice? Fairly masculine, is it not?"

"Perhaps yet I only intend to keep the three beginning letters," she declared. "My mid name rhymes with Bricius and akin to a water house. It shalt beest Bridgette."

"Bridgette," repeated Leak. "Bridgette Switch, I approve. Deign us a while with this subject aside. Then we talk of our alliance?"

"Nay! The final nameth, daemon."

"Very well. I might yet pulleth an image from thy pate."

"Another dissemble to scape and devour me?"

"Nay, I doth it from hither. Never thee mind. Privee, Sitteth upon the floor and close thy eyes. Concentrate on a past image of interest in thy life. I shalt pluck the bethought from remembrance to explore possibilities."

"Rings akin to demonic inventions."

"Do or not, I hast nowhere to hie this instant. Mayhap thou plaited an agreement anon?"

"Nay alliance," she replied. On the wooden floor, she closed her eyes to concentrate.

The daemon observed a pale vapor rise from the girl's forehead. As it drifted closer to Leak, the cloud formed a remnant of canvas. He smiled at the artistic depiction sketched in charcoal.

"Open thy eyes," he ordered, holding the image. "Does thou recognizeth yond art?"

"Tis the drawing once residing at the home of a retired sailor. In his time, that gent explored many faraway lands."

"Tis the Himalayan Mountain range. Wherefore doth thou suppose yond image cometh to mind?"

"Mayhap mine world is one big mountain range," she considered. "Nay, mine desire to beest the greatest upon the Earth."

"Grant a name representing thy ambitions, wench."

"A shortened version of the range. Hema!"

A brief surprise fell on the coven as the door bolt levitated from its cradles. As the young empusa stepped into the main hall, the others realized that Leak had used his vis to unseal the exit. From his far-off prison, the daemon threw his voice. Loud and understood, he proclaimed, "I present thy newest coven member, Hema Bridgette Switch."

A chant of "congratulations" erupted.

Chapter Eight: Renting VHS

The sound of my rasping breath faded as I sat up in bed. Flopping off the encased water, my sleepy body sought out the wall switch. The abrupt light was disorienting. When my vision recovered, I grabbed both notebook and pen before sitting on the carpet.

'My nightmare,' I scrolled with carefully constructed capitol letters. The evenly spaced paragraphs, that followed, described a wilderness scene taking place eight days before the explosive assassination of Lord Darnley, the great grandson of King Henry VII. If you're not familiar with this piece of history, it doesn't matter. My entry had nothing to do with British royalty and everything to do with witch burning and floating heads. Glancing back over the page in the progress journal, I discovered omitted details. The pen tip again made contact with paper, but my brown eyes habitually glanced across the room to the alarm clock.

"Oh Fob," I declared, dropping everything as I got up. "I'm going to be late!"

The bell tinkled above the door as I entered *Erotic Kingdom.* Sweat dripped from my scalp and I was treated with the usually pungent aroma that often lingered in the store's interior.

"Hey," I said to the man behind the counter.

"You're sweating in October," commented the rash-faced Tyler Then. I imagined he was trying to be funny, but the tone was hushed. Tyler commonly spoke like his nasal passages were blocked, combined with a slur. "Were you running late?"

Tyler had been sick for a while. Hearing his cough, I tried going along with his attempt at banter.

"A few minutes," I admitted while passing his location. The glass beneath displayed bongs, cigarette paper, and Amyl nitrate. This last product came in breakable popper or glass jars with a bb inside. It was sold under brand names like *Silver Bullet* or *Locker Room*. A handwritten sign claimed that the substance was sold as 'head cleaner' for electric equipment. It took less than a week of working at the adult bookstore to realize that the clientele was sniffing it to get a quick high.

"It's actually warm for this time of year," I added, carrying the small backpack past shelves of silicone toys, pornographic magazines, VHS rentals, and homosexual novels. At the far end of the room, I stepped through a door to a poorly lit office.

Within, the neglected walls and door frames exposed the building's century-and-a-half old office and storeroom. Beyond allowing people access to the restroom, management wasn't concerned with our opinion of the atmosphere. I placed my bag on the green desk, next to the coffee maker and adding machine.

On a nearby cutting board were fragments from the newest pornographic video purchases. Once a week, Bob Delbert, Co-owner and manager, would buy cheap VHS tapes from a traveling distributer. The covers would be cut down, laminated, given a rental price, purchase label, and late fee charge.

The backroom contained two other doors. The one, to the right of the entrance, had a black and white embossed symbol for a unisex restroom. Tacked to the other, located straight ahead, was a cardboard square. After my experience with taking the trash out that door, I made the sign. It depicted a falling stick figure. Above the image were the words *Caution: Drop off!*

I'd fallen fourteen feet onto several bags of garbage. Near the landing sight was a park were drunks frequented. I knew many of them and they were amused. Bob Delbert laughed as well. I suppose I might have healed, even if I hadn't landed on the other trash. Unfortunately, Ergerteine didn't mend humiliation the way it did human tissue.

"I'm taking off," declared Tyler. I nodded then followed him to the sales floor.

"Have a good one."

Tyler, in his striped golf shirt and hiked up jeans, reminded me of the geeky, upper middle-class kids from my high school days. His reddish-brown hair was evenly combed and pasted to his scalp, the same way Carver Kastleberg did in junior high. If not for thinner frames on his oversized reading glasses, I'd have reasoned that the two got fashion advice from the same bad source.

The entrance bell jingled as Tyler Then passed an incoming customer. It was Clarence Eggen, a regular customer. This guy reminded me of a chunky Bill Bixby. You know; the actor from that TV show where he turned into a big green dude.

"Tyler looks bad," I commented. "I hope he gets over whatever's ailing him."

"Probably not," Clarence responded, lingering in front of the counter. Sitting in the chair by the register, the look in his eyes made me uncomfortable. It was my job to be pleasant, but Clarence was interested in an activity that straight men aren't on board with. "I heard he was diagnosed with AIDS."

I was shocked. I'd heard how the virus had devastated the country but hadn't affected anyone I knew.

"Here. Give me ten in quarters," he stated, handing me currency. Tilted forward, his eyes glaring from the top of his head. "You want to go in the back and watch the movie with me."

"Nope," I declined and not for the first time. "I'm straight."

"Straight men only think they're straight," he replied. After an uncomfortably long moment of grinning and staring, Clarence picked the ten-dollar roll from the glass countertop. Turning, he walked up the carpeted step and into the other section of the store.

Beneath the cash register, monochrome video monitors showed his figure strolling to one of four video booths. Much as Clarence did over the next few hours, male customers would come to Erotic Kingdom and roam between the front room and the coin operated video booths. They weren't there for the movies. Their goal was to seek out other male interested in companionship. Though they denied it, the management of Delbert-Trevale knew all about it. Why else would they have cut square openings, commonly referred to as Glory Holes, between the insides of the booths.

As Clarence Eggen stepped out of view, I pondered why he presented himself so aggressively. The average gay men that entered the store were subtle. Most couldn't be distinguished from straight guys. If they thought someone might be gay, they struck up a carefully worded conversation. Most were apologetic and tried their best not to offend or frighten the other customers. Having had gay acquaintances through the years, I tried to be understanding. Casual-natured visitors were more in line with how normal heterosexuals hooked up.

Those like Clarence, sorry to say, would be in a category the most tolerant of people would find creepy.

I pulled out my journal from under the register and placed in the letter. I tried to read a few entries but kept being interrupted by entering clientele and wandering Clarence. I had given up by the time the first group of drinkers wandered in from the bars.

They loved to point and laugh at the adult toys. It was quite entertaining for them. Unfortunately, they frightened the real money spenders as they toured the store. There were three regulars at the time, and each moved to the VHS rental displays as the group walked back to the booths. The store's usual clientele preferred discretion. They didn't want steady lovers, family, or friends finding out about their supplementary pastime.

The last of the inebriated gawkers stumbled out of the store, passed by two women.

"I told you he'd be at work," December announced to my older sister. "You said he'd be out begging Kastleberg for forgiveness."

"Oh, Collie," Gypsie mocked, getting down on one knee. "Please take me back. I don't care if you have the body of a vulture and can give more wood to people than…"

"This," December finished, grabbing a rubber dildo from its shelf. Wiggling the purple object in my direction, my sisters laughed.

"Shut up," I responded as Gypsie got to her feet. Glancing to the VHS section, I noticed that the *regulars* appeared amused. "I'm kind of busy right now. Can you harass me later?"

"*Ferris Boner Gets Off, Fast Times at Rim Job High, Edward Penis Hands*; hilarious," Gypsie read as she perused video covers. "Wow, these prices are outrageous!"

"Yep," I admitted. "Good ol 'Bob likes to pay twenty bucks a tape then mark up the price to a hundred."

"Nice profit margin," Gypsie smiled.

"Unless you're the renter," I responded. "If friends walk off with your porn or the family dog uses them as chew toys, store policy is to bill you. With a three VHS maximum, after only a week, you owe Delbert-Trevale three hundred dollars."

"That's highway robbery," December announced, placing the cover of *Night of the Giving Head* back on the shelf. "Why doesn't he just convert to mainstream videos. The other video places get so much more business."

"I tried to tell that to Bob but he took it as a joke," I said. "Fob. I even drew him a possible floor plan."

"He must not know what he's doing. This place has been closed down four times and probably been owned by at least that many people," December claimed. "Seems to me, if pornography can't keep you in business for more than a few years, a stronger sales model is the solution."

"You're right. As much as I like this place, it'll never compete with the mainstream video market," replied Clarence. "This place will be a passing memory in a few years while the Blockbusters and Hy-Vee video outlets will be around in 2090."

December gave Clarence Eggen a stern look and it was obvious to me that she sensed the same uncomfortable aura he carried. She nodded with apprehension. Gypsie gave him a similar look as I tried to think of a different subject. The telephone rang.

"Hello, Erotic Kingdom, Hugo speaking. How may I help you? <pause> Hey, Mortimer. What's up <long pause> I see. <pause> Yeah. <pause> I get it," I claimed with disappointment in my eyes. <pause> "Bye."

"What was that about?" Gypsie asked.

"That was Mortimer Trevale, the other owner. He called to tell me that, starting in the morning, I have to open the store."

"That's going to be tough after working tonight. But, hey, it's just one time. You'll catch up with your sleep, bro."

"Instead of my usual seven to three AM, I'll be working a twelve-hour shift. I come in at eleven in the morning and Bob will replace me around eleven in the evening, depending on his schedule. It turns out that Tyler's condition was worse than I thought."

"I told you he contracted AIDS," replied Clarence. The other regulars nodded their agreement. "Mortimer's known for a while."

"And they weren't looking for a replacement? Fobs," December griped. "They barely pay you over minimum wage now, Hugo. To ask you to work overtime, for weeks, with no extra compensation is too much. They should at least give you a longer lunch break."

"Agreed and I have to take my lunch on the clock. I asked about going out for lunch once and Bob said, 'you just sit there all night now.'" Glancing at the backroom monitor, I continued.

"Working here isn't a picnic. When our customers aren't making advances toward me, they're telling the bosses that I hate gay people."

The *regulars* stopped making eye contact.

"Those aren't even the biggest store lies. I constantly catch Bob and Mortimer telling me whoppers about the most insignificant things. I don't doubt, for an instance, that they could have had a replacement before now," I complained. "I've been called to the store for a break-in and one time when someone set off the fire alarm. You should see what I have to do to clean this dump after the closing paperwork and bank receipts are done. It's revolting."

"Quit," said December but Gypsie hushed her.

"Bob and Mortimer live over thirty miles from town. I'm the one that keeps this place going and have basically been store manager since my first month. I don't even get a lousy title to show for my effort. Oh, I did get a quarter raise after nine months, bringing me to $3.50 an hour. I don't know why I do it. There's no amount of money that…!"

"Then quit."

"Shut up, Sis! How's he supposed to pay his rent," Gypsie asked December. "Change the subject. Hugo, tell me about this harpy."

"Harpia," I corrected.

"Everyone knows it's a harpy, Hugo," interjected Clarence. His eyes followed two *regulars* as they moved up the step to the other half of the store. He placed a laminated cover for *The Adventures of Buckaroo Bangaguy* on its display before following the men to the quarter booths.

"How do we know there's only one," asked Gypsie.

"And what if she decides to fly someplace else and start all over again?" questioned December. "We need to find Colleen and drive a stake through her heart."

"That's vampires, Sis," corrected Gypsie.

"Whatever," December responded.

I found the *Harpia* section in the pages of *Tools for Practical Witchcraft.* During the monstrum discussion, December changed the topic.

"Oh, I saw your flame going into Bootlegs."

Separated by an alley, *Bootleg's Gin Joint* was a dance bar and restaurant on the same block as the store.

"My flame," I questioned, readying myself for an insult.

"If he has a flame, it wouldn't be that freak

Colleen," Gypsie interjected. "I don't get what you ever saw in her."

"Other than sex," December stated. "No, I meant Becca Webb."

I deny it but was unconvincing. Especially when you're being teased, it's hard to ignore feelings of attraction.

"Oh, come on, Hugo," Gypsie stated. "We've known about your crush on Becca since high school."

"The harpia is said to be the living personification of storm winds," I read, trying to ignore her. "What's that supposed to…?"

Breaking free of the upper door spring, the entrance burst open. A forceful wind took the tiny bell and chucked it into the wall next to the backroom. Wood display shelves toppled, merchandise was airborne, and my sisters fell to the carpet.

I ducked behind the worst place to avoid a powerful wind, the glass counter. Through the front, I watched the adult toys squirm along the floor like bizarre worms then stop. The wind had abruptly died.

"A tornado," someone outside questioned. There were multiple voices expressing their astonishment for the sudden change in breeze. Among the conversations, I targeted a name. Becca.

A woman was talking about two ladies who had been just outside the bar up the street then, after the gust, vanished.

"I know one of them was Becca Webb," another voice proclaimed. "They were just swept away."

Amongst the clutter in the store, I finally found both my notebook and the letter beneath a stack of *Juggs* and *Hustler* magazines. I turned to the last sentence I'd read as my sisters looked over my shoulders. Both were startled when I slammed the volume closed and handed it to Gypsie.

"Hugo?"

Determination drove me back to my workstation. I lifted the phone received and tapped in Mortimer's number. While waiting for a voice on the other end of the line, I shouted, "The store's closed! Get out!"

Chapter Nine: Tempus Amplius

On July tenth, 1567, Empusa Hema found herself crouched between a canopy headboard and a floral tapestry. Woven into the center of the wall hanging was a fence enclosing a pale unicorn. Hema thought it appeared forlorn; a feeling she shared while reconsidering the decision to conceal herself among Mistress Dacian's belongings.

More than five months had passed since joining the coven. She recalled one of the members of the sisterhood dropping a bound stack of paper (made from linen rags) into her hands. This was common practice that each witch have her own book of maleficia. Their mistress made certain that they were all proficient in reading, writing, and basic mathematics. The trouble with the book, however, was that Dacian left it up to the individual witch to obtain their own maleficia. This, Hema discovered, was impossible because her new sisters coveted their findings.

There were two exceptions. The new member was given instruction to perform a maleficia by Mistress Dacian herself. It had no title or incantation, just a few hand signals and a slight amount of vis. She had to be between twenty-four and thirty-six inches from the target. On the occasion it worked, this maleficia would cause an object to move no more than a few feet. Though the pupil was about as likely to succeed at casting this maleficia as winning a coin toss, she gave it a name. *Auxilium* (which meant *Help*) was good for acquiring the saltshaker during a table meal or untying someone's shoes.

Empusa Juana (*Juana Quin Shang*), seeing that Hema had no maleficia written down, agreed to give her one. She laughed as she scribed it into her tome. To perform Juana's witchery, one would place a whole potato in a bowl of water. Placing it upon a window ledge, an incantation was recited. If the potato were properly watered and care was taken, the caster's wandering lover would return as much as a year later.

Empusa Hema had never been romantically entangled. So, like Juana, found the book addition to be a pitiful waste of space.

Most of the pages of Hema's book were devoted to describing the monstrum she'd encountered. Her fingers flipped to a drawing of a horned horse. Hema had seen it one misty morning in Laingaham square. The other witches made fun and doubted her unicorn sighting. It wasn't difficult to shrug off their denials. Hema's trouble was ignoring her lack of maleficia. To her, it represented deficient progress in her ability to master her new life. Laying against a hay bale, used as filler for each of the witch's beds, she moped.

While contemplating, a few sisters entered the

hall. They couldn't see her on the opposite side of the bedding.

"Wulfhild quoth so," claimed Empusa Juana. "The one-witch covets her maleficia within an ingraft handkerchief; the embroidered one the lady so oft possesses. Tis ingenious."

"I wouldst love to tryeth such with mine tome," admitted Empusa Abu. "It wouldst beest much easier to bear. Doth thou regard Sorcha with such knowledge?"

"Doubtful," Hema heard Empusa Preciosa comment. "Besides, the way Dacian transports her folio is of nay importance. The powerful maleficia matters high-lone. I wouldst beest grateful for a glance."

"A single word or phrase wouldst not satisfy a beldam," stated Abu.

"Nor a single leaf," added Juana. "A night or more wouldst beest required to explore its mysteries."

"Of course, but how would you get the maleficia from the cloth?" Hema thought. Considering her current location, the answer became apparent.

In Dacian's chamber, the young witch thumbed through pages of sketches. It was her attempt to fight sleep, yet it overtook her anyway. She woke to the voice of Sorcha Kaenylm.

"The lady shalt beest hither anon." Through a gap in the headboard, Hema saw Sorcha near the entrance but couldn't find a second person. "Thou wilt encave me. Hie."

Bits of green burst into existence, encasing the speaker. The spy recognized the particles as vis. When it faded, Sorcha's image was gone. Hearing walking across to one side of the room, it was apparent that Sorcha was still present. She'd called on something to make herself invisible or, at least, the vis necessary to acquire that state.

"Why wouldst Empusa Sorcha hide within Mistress Dacian's cubiculo," Hema wondered. Sorcha was so powerful, compared to the others in the coven. Was there a spell in the one-witch's collection that she desired? "Mayhap she's hither for common reasons?"

The entrance opened and a figure stepped within. Though containing a hearth, several randomly placed candles, and five stands, only the chamber's center candelabra was lit. Approaching a chair, Hema saw Dacian: the one-witch.

"I shall beest conjuring in mine chambers, Empusa Godleaf," Dacian announced as she shed a purple cloak. Godleaf, who held the honored title of Lady Chamberlain, closed the double doors from the outside. "Be certain there art nay disturbances."

Dacian dropped the cloak over the chair then strolled to the bed. Hema knew that Godleaf would move the castoff article to one of the wardrobes when appropriate. Because of her title, she was responsible for items and events concerning the bedchamber and Dacian.

From a hidden gown pocket, the one-witch removed a circular gray piece of cloth. The spy recognized the letters *U.C.D.* (standing for *Una Crina Dacian*) embroidered along its edge.

At one corner of the chamber, Dacian removed a leather-bound tome from the bookcase then walked back to her bed. As she sat, the copy of *Biblia Vulgata* could be seen. Opening it, Dacian placed the cloth on a page then closed the volume. Hema's eyes widened as the object noticeably altered into a completely different book. She made out the words *Mittentes Praestigiis* (Latin for *Casting Witchcraft*). Holding her ink quill in one hand, the spy waited for her mistress to put the *Mittentes Praestigiis* where she could get an unobstructed view.

"Sorcha," raged Mistress Dacian. As the book dropped to the bed, both palms thrust forward. Vis crackled into an electric charge. The outline of a dagger appeared then two limbs. The spy behind the bed understood its meaning.

With Sorcha Kaenylm exposed, Dacian's palm lightning erupted. The force thrust the adversary across the chamber and into a red curtain. Directly behind the fabric, the wall was solid, living wood. Sorcha's shoulders hit hard and, between that and the initial jolt, her insides were in agony.

"How dareth thou presume to enter this private chamber. To what endeth, wench? Thou hath arrived to assassinate thee? Shalt thou stealeth mine rightful throne in the bargain? This shalt not beest permitted, brigand," yelled Dacian. "There is but one mistress of this coven and yond is mine own distinction!"

Hema glanced away from the conflict to see the closed book on the bed. Fingers cast *Auxilium* and, successful, flipped the leather cover and a sixpence worth of pages. Jotting down the paper, she stopped momentarily. The purpose of the maleficia registered. With a deep breath, the spy dipped her quill and inked the final paragraph.

Sorcha had crawled over onto her stomach and lifted herself into a dog-like stance. Mistress Dacian stood beside the wood framed bed with her legs locked and fingers poised for another mystic attack.

"A haggish epithet shalt be placed upon conspirators in defiance of thy mistress." Her volume dropped as a tall figure materialized at her enemy's right side. "Misanthropes?"

A demonic man smiles warmly at Dacian while reaching down to Sorcha's wrist. Vis passed from his palm through the mystically damaged frame. With only her sclera showing, the head quaked followed by the spine and limbs. When she stopped, the companion guided Sorcha to a standing position. The traitor's calm, unaffected demeaner disturbed her mistress.

"Thou art acquainted with Leak," said Sorcha. "We hast decided to work as one."

With open left-handed motions and thrusting three right fingers forward, the one with recited another maleficia. Within a digit of her extended hand, a series of wiggling lines revealed themselves. Like missiles, they thrust into the treacherous empusa.

"Zookers! Nay," she screamed as four snake-like worms blazed through her clothing, charring the pale flesh within. Struggling with blistered fingers, Sorcha hit the far curtain and back onto the floor. "Fire worms! Thou morbid harlot!"

The moment her mistress' fire worm-attack began, Hema performed her newly acquired maleficia. She was certain that her voice was not detected over Sorcha's screams. After the final word of the incantation, the room became hyper silent.

"It worked," Hema shouted, coming out from behind the headboard. Leaping over a dark cube shaped chest, decorated with a moon, sun, and a multitude of stars, she saw Sorcha. Her hands clutched one of the giant worms. More grubs and flames protruded from her chest, yet nothing flickered nor writhed.

Everything was locked between motion. Dacian's limbs were lowered slightly from when she'd cast the last attack. She was otherwise unmoving. Leak's gaze was focused on the head of her bed, yet he was inanimate too. Before the maleficia, his neck had dropped slightly from the head. Now a gap showed inner gore as though he had been abandoning the body. In the center of the room, the lit candelabra wicks stood a motionless yellow and red. Solid smoke connecting them to the tree-limb ceiling like strings from a child to a kite.

Jumping over a cassone (a painted chest), the young witch considered a maleficia that allowed time to stop time, added a few minutes, then started from where it left off.

"Additional moments? I shalt entitle it, *Tempus Amplius,*" she determined while picking *Mittentes Praestigiis* from the blanket. "I barely hadst the vis yond maleficia required. Shalt I counterfeit yond book by motion's awakening?"

Hema determined that copying the book's contents would work better from somewhere else. She ran to the double doors, passing a group of wood cushioned bench and four chairs. Empusa Godleaf and Dionysia stood in the hall by the center fire. The flames stood like colorful ice while the witches were frozen in mid of conversation. Clutching both door handles, Hema felt assured that she might avoid these women before *Tempus Amplius* ended.

The contact of the closed passage sparked an explosion of sound and motion. Flames flickered as Leak's torso and limbs flopped onto the planks below. The head, levitating, swerved its steel gray eyes toward the double entry. There was a brief instance of confusion followed by the daemon shifting in Dacian's direction.

"To be so emboldened as to believe thou couldst collar Leak," he raged with his long tongue flopping down among slimy guts. "Thee shalt regret thy aggression, doxy *(a promiscuous woman)*. I shall find glee in the taste of thy carn *(flesh and meat)*."

Dacian's attention was split between the daemon's threat and a potential assault from her empusa. An undetected force, like a boulder rolling from a hilltop, shoved her off her feet. The rear of the mistress' skull crashed through a standing mirror, slicing every inch of exposed skin.

Sorcha had used a maleficia to ice over her fiery worms. Though in agony, she pulled herself into a sitting position with legs spread. Through burnt eyelids, she made out the other witch on the opposite side of the chamber. Leak's assault had lacerated Dacian's smooth features, exposing the coven's initiation flaying, yet the one-witch struggled along the floor.

Sorcha fumed as her mistress began another incantation. Watching the mystic gestures, the empusa decided on a maleficia that might break the woman's fingers. Both recited Latin with nimble moving digits but Sorcha was confident that her attack would win out. Shock covered her seared face when every shard of the damaged mirror rose. Her concentration faded as the glass shot in her direction. Magic fizzled as a shard tore into Sorcha

Jane Kaenylm's arm, followed by many more. Vis scattered as the deceased body slumped and stopped moving.

Leak snarled at the sight of the punctured corpse. His seething expression moved a few inches toward Dacian then stopped. Both had become as inanimate as the deceased. The entrance opened without noise and Hema rushed inside the bed chamber.

Chapter Ten: Beef with Becca

The white Mercury Cougar drove off the concrete path and onto the dirt trail. Gypsie shut off the engine and stepped from the station wagon.

"Is it safe leaving it here?" December questioned, getting out of the seat behind the driver's position. She had grabbed two flashlights from the glove box.

"The arboretum is closed at night," Gypsie stated as she took one of the lights. "Just inside these woods is the best place to hide it from passing security."

"I still think it was unfair of mom to give you her old car while I have to ride a bike everywhere," I complained, walking along side my sisters.

"She needed a trade-in. I convinced her that

trading my car worked out for both of us," Gypsie confessed. "The station wagon is only eight years old."

"Hugo. Was it a good idea to lock the store early without even doing the bank receipts?" questioned December as we moved deeper into the wilderness.

"Mortimer knows that I quit," I said. "Putting the cash in the safe and locking the store was reasonable, considering the way he and Bob treated me."

"They're fobs, bro," Gypsie commented. Her light reflected off a racoon's retina as it scurried around a hawthorn thicket. The beam reangled back to the trail. "Now. Are you sure Becca Webb is out here?"

"She should be," I answered. "The harpia is supposed to perch here in the evening."

"I'm not feeling sick," December admitted. "Are you positive?"

"No, I'm not an expert on the arial migratory habits of the common harpia," came my acrimonious response. "I don't know why we haven't gotten sick or if Becca is out here. The next time someone we know is scooped up in a windstorm by a creature only talked about in myths,

I'll try to think of a better plan."

"Well, someone's a bit moody," said December.

"Yeah," agreed Gypsie. "Maybe our little brother likes this girl more than he wants to admit."

"Dalton is your little brother," I corrected. "And shut up."

After a lengthy walk, December announced, "I think this is it."

"How can you be sure," questioned Gypsie. I looked up but could barely see the outline of the tree. Gypsie aimed her beam ten feet up the trunk, exposing a man-like shape beneath a thick branch. The uneasy curve of wood in the form of a gaping mouth caused her to lift the light. On the upper side of that limb, talons held a large bird in place. When the illumination explored further, however, Colleen Kastleberg's head sneered down at us. Her lips opened, allowing a repetitive caw to escape.

"Help me," a voice pleaded. The other light moved thirty feet past the harpia to discover Becca. "Whoever you are, get me down. Please!"

"It's okay, Becca," I claimed. "We're coming to get you."

"Hugo?" she responded. "Hurry up before that thing comes back."

"It never left," a feminine voice claimed.

"Stop it, December. You're going to make things worse," Gypsie proclaimed. "Are you stoned, bro? What makes you think you can climb all the way up there and bring your damsel in destress here without getting your eyes scratched out or falling out of the tree?"

"I didn't say anything," confessed December.

"I've got to try, sis," I responded. "In the book, it claims that the harpia has to add a person to the tree every day it exists here. If the sun comes up, Becca's an instant victim."

"Can't we just free her later," asked December. "With the others?"

"There's no known maleficia that can reverse the victim's wooden state," said someone.

"What's a maleficia," considered Gypsie, turning her light toward our sister. "Wait. That wasn't December's voice."

"That's what I was trying to tell you," December exclaimed.

We were taken aback when four burning sources suppressed our flashlights. This was caused by the abrupt igniting of kerosene tipped rods extending from the trail soil. Four headless men held bows in our direction. The arrows were notched and ready to be released. I half expected a few ewai to be wandering the woods since our last encounter. Yet, for some unexplained reason, I was thunderstruck by the presence of a woman in a crimson robe. Pulling down her hood, we discovered the face of Wilona Schuster.

"It seems you've fallen into our trap, Mr. Grazer," Willo announced. Looking up the yew, details were blacked out beyond the reflection of Colleen's eyes. "You weren't as tough an adversary as my mistress purported."

"If you work for Switch, who are you," I inquired. "You're no more Willo than that thing in the tree is Colleen Kastleberg."

The woman laughed and, while my sisters and I watched, her skin distorted bronze into a milk tone. Straight dark hair bunched along her head, forming distinctly brown braids. The eyes within her oval face gazed green instead of the previous yellow-brown.

"Satisfied?"

"I don't get it. Who are you supposed to be?" December asked. "What's your beef with Becca Webb?"

"I could care less about the stupid girl." Her thin frame moved forward, high shoulders giving the appearance of a woman much taller than five foot ten inches. "My job is to protect the harpia. If that requires a few extra deaths than…"

"Empusa Brynhild, pardon," said an ewai. It held its weapon toward the ground as the exposed chest. "Your servant has arrived."

"What's so important about a homicidal freak-bird?" December questioned as Heart Seacord stepped from the edge of the illumination. She carried a potted flower. "What…what's with the plant."

"It's what she was sent to obtain," claimed Brynhild. "That flower means that your friend, Vince, is no longer a threat."

"I cast the spell exactly as you requested," Heart announced, placing the decorative container on the ground. From the potting soil, stood a foot and a half long stem with a burgundy flower head. The brown center, comprised of seeds, measured three inches in diameter. "It was hard to carry but it's intact."

"Are they saying that sunflower is CIA Vince," wondered Gypsie.

"It was," the witch confessed then brought her foot down on the plant. The stem snapped. "Which of your sisters will be next. Either would make a good daisy."

"I'm going to bust this witch-broad in her shapeshifting nose," Gypsie announced. The armed ewai brought his arrow tip closer to her.

Caw! Everyone on the ground looked up to see the shadow of the harpia swooping from its perch. Becca had her arms around its neck as the monstrum erratically soared overhead. Her legs swayed as the great bird changed direction.

"She'll strangle it," yelled Brynhild. "Kill Becca Webb!"

CRACK! The echoing sound was followed by Becca and the winged beast plummeting into the grass. The headless ewai sprinted to their landing spot. December grabbed my arm, stopping me from running to help Becca.

CRACK! A tongue hung out of one of their chests as it spun then struck the path. A moment later and the ewai was dead. The others, realizing their predicament, tried to locate the sniper with the tip of their arrow.

"Is that thing going to fall," I questioned, seeing the yew tree shake. Gypsie shoved me and December off the path. Heart ran behind her. The huge tree had lost its firm appearance, slowly wobbling its swollen parts downward, toward the spectators.

"What's going on around here," Brynhild queried as the yew gradually deconstructed. Searching for the harpia, Brynhild discovered that Becca was laying on top of an ashen substance. Though vaguely shaped like a bird, the object resembled the swollen substance from the yew. Bits flaked into the night as the witch grabbed Becca's dark hair.

"You!" Empusa Brynhild complained. "This is your doing!"

"That thing kidnapped me!" Becca retorted as she pulled out of the witch's grasp. Most of the tree lay among the grass and soil, shedding its former bark. "How am I at fault for any of this?"

CRACK! CRACK! CRACK! Brynhild Aelfweard looked back to find that the other ewai were lifeless. The broken flower still lay nearby.

"Heart!" she concluded. Seacord, who had been huddled near us, stood up straight and faced the empusa. "Vince Sorum Jr. isn't dead. He's out there in the dark! You betrayed the coven."

"Did you really think that, after all your mistress put me through, that I'd be cool with screwing over Hugo, his family or their friends," Heart questioned. "And, while you may have seen it as a warped kind of irony, I was never going to turn another human being into a potted flower. That's just sick!"

"Let me show you the depths of sickness, whore," raged Brynhild. As fingers gestured, the next words from her mouth were Latin.

Heart clenched her teeth and winced. She'd expected a mystic bombardment. Instead, the incantation was cut short by another .50 caliber blast. CRACK!

We had barely accepted that the danger had passed when a man with a rifle stepped into the light.

"Vince," I realized. "You're not a broken flower. That's great, man."

"You really saved our bacon," December added. Turning to the others. "Don't you think…"

Gypsie, Becca, and Heart weren't looking in our direction. Their attention was focused on a newcomer.

Unless you count a photo in *Tools for Practical Witchcraft*, I'd only seen Mistress Switch a few times. Every encounter with her left goosebumps along my neck and shoulders. This time seemed worse. Tiny hairs rose along my back as she scowled at the dissipating yew. Vis flowed behind her, making patterns resembling an oncoming storm.

"My harpia," she said in a low tone.

Oh, I'm still 423 years ahead of myself. I forgot to finish telling you about Dacian's battle with Sorcha and the daemon Leak.

Empusa Hema had copied every maleficia contained in Dacian's book before returning to the room. There she discovered that the coven leader had cast mystic circles to ensnare the floating head. Noticing Hema, Dacian gave a speech designed to encourage the young girl into staying loyal. Her words were those of a friend and mentor.

"Loyalty," Mistress Switch recalled responding. "I did love mine mother. Yet, as much as I hath felt for her, I adored mine Ealdemodor Wilmina doubly so. Thou did allow her to sear! There wast despair at the hands of villagers yet none compareth to ye coven's sting. The atrocious acts thee hast made me doth! Una Crina Dacian, matriarch of the contemptable, thou high-lone hadst the ability to forbear it all! For thy lack of empathy and wanton wickedness, I end thou."

Dacian, through a lacerated mouth, laughed. Hema took a deep breath then exposed a familiar gray handkerchief. The laughter continued but no longer bubbled out of Dacian. It was Leak, who watched as Hema used the mistress' own recipe to convert the magic cloth into an enormous collection of paper.

"'Tis mine, wandought *(a weak person)*!" Dacian barked, standing.

"Retain thou maleficia," Hema proclaimed, tossing it into the witch's arms. "'Tis a representation of thou at the instant of mine family's murder. Like thou, it shalt not provide aid."

With her free hand, Dacian started a maleficia from memory. Hema wasn't swayed. She had already done her groundwork. All that was required was a gesture. With a flick of her hand, the index finger unleashed a beam of red light. It passed through both the book and Dacian like a giant razor blade.

When it dissipated, everything from Dacian's waist to her toes, fell forward. The lacerated expression was one of astonishment. Then, as if just discovering gravity, the upper half fell and landed on the cauterized end. She looked like the top half intended to console the fallen legs and buttocks. Eventually aware that it couldn't survive without the other section, the face fell to the floor with one arm laying across the left leg.

"Impressive display," Leak grinned. His

human appearance reformed beneath the head. "I did select Sorcha only due to thee procrastinating our mutual partnership. I seeth anon yond lady was a cumberground *(worthless individual)*. Let us reconsider a union."

"Nay. Thou truly did crave freedom. An admirable goal except thy resolve did include mine betrayal as thou did plot likewise against Dacian," Hema retorted. "Alas, I madeth potential offers to thy princes and other palmy monstrum."

"I shall doth worse than betrayal if thou do not release me, crooked-nose wench!"

"Doubtful. As part of mine binding with thy masters, I informed them of thy treachery. They had a pact with Mistress Dacian. Thy conduct is like to any of the dark princes breaking that contract. I return thou to Hell to answer for thy treason, coxcomb *(Foolish or vain person)*."

"Gip!"

After a brief incantation, Leak and the circles collapsed into the floor, vanishing from view. Hema reached down and clutched Dacian's hair. As she drug half of a corpse to the exit, lingering vis floated to her like flies to light.

"I didst restrain a demonic insurrection instigated by Empusa Sorcha and, in self-preservation, vanquish Una Crina Dacian," she stated, pulling the hair upward. "I, Hema Bridgette Switch, claim mine rightful position as ruler of this coven. Any in disagreement may shareth the fate of the dead."

Mistress Switch would, later, present Dacian's body to the daemon of the witch's sabbath.

Chapter Eleven: Ignis Anulus

While the rest of us keep volumes of reference books safely tucked away on a shelf, HB Switch modified Dacian's hankie trick. How cool is it to have your own *encyclopedia of the weird* accessible anywhere you go simply by writing a letter? I suppose you're wondering how I know so much about Switch's life. It's all in her book.

On that subject, I was telling you about the early morning of October 8th, 1990.

"Empusa Brynhild was one of the few sisters I kept after taking over the coven," Switch lamented. Standing in a red gown, reminiscent of something worn by a fairytale princess, the witch took time to examine the devastation of the yew tree and her servants. When her attention shifted, that gaze scrutinized each survivor. Midnight eyes stopped at Heart Seacord. "This has your stench."

"What are you going to do," Heart inquired with stammered vocals.

"Eliminate minor annoyances," she replied while spinning in the direction of Cadadrius Agent Vince Sorum Jr. Her left index finger pointed. I saw that the ring on that finger had heated to the intensity of hot lava. "All of them."

Vince had her pale face within his rifle sights. He'd just switched off the safety when his face wrinkled, and the gun left his clutches. Both palms went to his sides as the agent bellowed in agony. I'll never forget that sound as fire burst from his head and shoulders.

"God, no," December said as the body incinerated before us. "Evil fob, you killed him!"

Ignoring the comment, Hema Switch turned her deadly ring in my direction. A wave of heat covered my flesh. It was like walking from a cold area of a room, directly over an active heat register.

Before the heatwave blistered, Heart interceded by flicking a wrist toward Switch. The mistress' large band slid off her hand. She fumbled for it, but it maneuvered between digits and into the grass.

"*Auxilium*?" Beneath her large brim hat, Switch scanned the vegetation. She didn't locate the ring. An incantation formed on her lips.

"Don't bother," Heart declared. Everyone stared, wondering where the comment had been directed.

"What have you done," her mistress scowled. Vaguely, at the edge of the illuminated ground, I saw something resembling a cylinder. At first, I thought it was made of fireflies, but it was too late in the season. Besides, the substance was smaller, green bits of faint illumination.

"Vis," Gypsie deduced.

Sure enough. Fumbling, but lovesick, Heart had figured out a way to drain the most powerful being I'd ever met. Anxious, Switch reached into the gown's hidden compartments. The first item she brought forth was a candle. Light flashed around it then the object joined the world of lost things. There were other items but, each time one was revealed, it suffered the same fate.

"What is this treachery, cursing all of my charms," Switch complained after losing a silver coin. The sixpence held the visage of Elizabeth the first with the hammered year of 1567. "I underestimated you, misanthrope."

"Even after all the torment, I'd still have forgiven you," Heart stated, emptying the sunflower pot. "But you won't leave Hugo alone. You know how I feel about him, but you just can't help yourself!"

"Heart, everything I did was for your own good," Switch insisted. "You're a witch, a child of the dark arts. It's not healthy to walk around with your romantic delusions."

"Love is not a delusion, Mistress," Heart explained, stepping within two yards of her mistress and dropping the pot. "Just because he doesn't share my feelings doesn't make them any less real."

"I see that now," Switch claimed as Heart mumbled Latin. Though we were unsure of the outcome, curiosity brought the rest of us closer. "Now, I must correct my mistake by ending you."

"At the risk of repeating myself, don't bother," Heart claimed as Switch created gestures in the air. "Not a single speck of vis will come to your aid. I've cut off your reserve."

"That can only be done with maleficia that I created," Switch explained. "I only recently worked it out. How could you know about it?"

"Rest your tired limbs," Heart insisted, pointing at the bowl. Inside was a few inches of soil. Though painful to watch, Switch contorted and altered until she became nothing more than a stem with a single bulb. Its open peddles formed a black hood with an interior white star. Heart sniffed it before turning to the others.

"She reminds me of *Alcea Rosea Nigra*," Heart said to me. I stared as one does when he believes the other person might be insane. How else should I have responded to what she'd done? "The black Hollyhock."

"Didn't you say that you'd never do that," reminded Becca.

"Mistress Switch would have never stopped. You'd have all suffered and eventually died by her wrath," Heart responded. "Of everyone in this world, she deserved this fate."

"How did you take her power," I asked.

"I'd been in *Tools for Practical Witchcraft* before. I'd witnessed those pages without her knowledge. Returning to human form would have only suited my mistress temporarily. That's where the maleficia *Tempus Amplius* came in handy. I used it to give myself an opportunity to catch up on other potential conjurings. Ever allowing me access to that book was her undoing," she explained. "Understand, Lovely Hugo. Switch's hatred for you was so intense that we'd have both ended up as plants."

"You weren't working with the other witch," Gypsie questioned.

"They needed to believe as much. Instead, I aligned myself with Vince Sorum. We initially planned to shoot them all and let the CIA take care of the corpses."

"Was killing Vince part of your plan," added Gypsie.

"*Ignis Anulus*, that I never expected," Heart assured them. "You must believe that I'd never seen a fire ring until now. My wish was to help Vince; to rescue you all. If I'd known sooner, I'd have cast my first maleficia sooner."

"I believe Heart," I announced.

"Good. Though I know we'll never be together," Heart insisted. "I hope we can continue to be friends, Hugo."

"I like you but you're right," I confessed. Standing behind my sisters, Becca gave a slight smile. I don't know if her grin was intended for me, but it did cause my heart to flutter. "We're just too different."

"I couldn't be in your life anyway," Heart announced. "To keep the coven from bothering your family, I must go back and take my place as the leader."

"Are you sure," December asked, affected.

"Unless you think you're up to it," Heart asked. "Switch implied that, someday, you might join the sisterhood."

"I'm no witch, lady," December insisted.

"Then that's that," Heart concluded. "*Vale.*"

A cloud of smoke ignited all around and when it faded, the witch was gone. The column of vis had also gone missing.

"That weird woman is willing to sacrifice the rest of her life out of love for you, Hugo," Becca said. "What is it that makes you so irresistible?"

"Wouldn't know," I admitted. The whole question made me uncomfortable because I've never seen myself in that way. "Can we get out of here?"

"There's one last order of business," Gypsie announced, staring at the black flower. "She's NOT coming back."

Converged on the potted flower, Gypsie was surprised to find that a white leather Reebok had knocked over the plant. Becca Webb stomped on the flower, mashing its petals and stem into pulp.

"Fob, girl," responded Gypsie. "I guess after your ordeal with the harpy, you deserved to be the one to knock off the wicked witch."

"Harpia," I corrected. My eyes caught the remains of the fallen yew and it brought back memories.

"You look like you might cry, Hugo," declared December. "I know you and Vince were friends but I never…"

"And Kastleberg," Gypsie reminded her.

"Yeah." Head down, my eyelids struggled with a tear. I contemplated, "What am I going to tell Carver?"

My frame shook as moisture formed at the edges of my eyelids. I know that Colleen and I could never have worked out our problems. Even so, I loved her once.

A set of arms embraced me. At first, I thought my sisters had dropped the tough act. I knew that somewhere inside every Grazer was a heart no different than any other human being. Was this the morning, as the sun peaked just below the trees, that they expressed mercy over my anguish?

No. That's not the way the Grazer's Mongolian horde interacted.

I looked up to find that Becca had stepped up. Her arms held me firmly, signaling that my feelings of loss were valid. I learned that a person could show strong, all the while showing their warmer side.

If she hadn't been there, I'd more likely have gotten a slug in the arm and told to stop being such a girl.

-

It's Monday night, December 31st and a new year will be here in a few minutes. Outside the bay windows, snow is impeding people as they go about traveling to work or home.

I decided to break my two-month sobriety and celebrate with a six pack of wine coolers. It was a bad idea. I don't know if the alcohol went bad or it was psychosomatic but that first sip was horrible! After tossing the open cooler in the trash, I took the other five to the neighbors upstairs.

Since then, I'd sat alone in the apartment. My thoughts shuffled through images. Dalton was likely working on a political campaign. Gypsie was out drinking with friends. I couldn't imagine what activities Zeke and December are up to. My mind went to Colleen Kastleberg. Because her son saw me as responsible for the death of both parents, I wasn't permitted at Colleen's funeral. My sisters and I showed up anyway but stayed far from the actual service.

While there, I gave Heart's letter to

December. She seems to be the most responsible pick and I give up. I never want to see another monstrum, witch, or strange occurrence again. I just wanted to settle down with a wonderful girl and live a normal life. The trouble was that I haven't seen that girl since that morning in October.

If you've never been in love, I don't expect you to understand. When you hurt so much over a missed love, you're likely to do most anything to get them back. It was the wrong approach, but I figured it was harmless. What am I talking about? Before I gave December access to all those spells… Oh, sorry. Magical people call them maleficia. Before I did that, I copied one entitled *Amor Annuum.*

I couldn't shrug the feeling that something was missing from my life. It had to be Becca! I was so sure that, before the day was over, I placed a potato in a bowl of water. Reciting the incantation, I was convinced it wouldn't work. The fobbing spud would die on the windowsill in the dead of winter. Right? Then again, a fragment of hope reminded me that *Amor Annuum* came straight from Switch's book.

The spud didn't die. Instead, as I watered it and spoke the words each day, it grew. During the first few weeks of January, I discovered roots had sprouted from the bottom. By the end of the month, a decent amount of foliage had formed. Surprised at its progress, I would move it on especially bitter days and return it to the sunniest window whenever possible.

Anyone that noticed it would warn, "If you don't transplant it in soil, the potato will rot and die."

More than once, I considered it but, because the maleficia never indicated using soil, I avoided the temptation.

The morning of July 5th, I was mystified at the potato's ability to survive. After placing it in the bathroom window, I got dressed for my dish washer job. I'd just buttoned my orange-red checkered shirt when the knocking began. Stepping to the door, I clipped my plastic *Pizza Cabana* nametag over the left pocket. Turning the handle and shoving, I expected to find a drunk, magazine salesperson, or a Jehovah's Witness.

No. My body got all giddy as I recognized the person standing on the landing. That smile was unmistakable. Was she prettier than I remembered?

"Becca."

We dated throughout the summer and, by fall, weren't interested in being with anyone else.

Unconvinced that the spud had brought us together, I loathed the potato plant. I was certain that tossing it in the garbage would end the experiment. My doubt concerned the connection between Becca and the plant. Would destroying the potato extinguish our romance? The weak part of me didn't want to find out.

Yet, by the end of that week, I had stopped speaking the incantation. A few days after, my obstinance won out and I ripped the plant apart.

I desperately needed to know if sweet Becca loved me or if she was under Switch's spell. It was a painful couple of weeks, worrying that she'd leave, but it hadn't happened. It turned out that *Amor Annuum* hadn't forced Becca Webb to love me. It had been designed exactly as the recipe detailed; to bring one's love interest back into their life.

"Thank God."

Epilogue: Diaper Duty

"She can't stand me," I said. I had my progress journal open on the coffee table. The date read July 17th, 1992, and I'd just glued a four-month-old article to the left page. "She doesn't like my family, my job, or even the church we go to."

"That's not true, Honey," Becca explained

from another room. "She hates most of your siblings. She likes your mom…and Dalton."

A concert ticket was stuck next to the *Tokeca Journal* clipping. The article was about the recent death of shock comedian Sam Kinison. I'd kept the ticket because it was one of the few comedy performances I'd attended. Gluing it in my journal deemed appropriate since it represented his last Iowa show. Closing the cover, I countered Becca's last remark.

"That's because she thinks Dalton has a respectable job!"

A knock stopped my train of thought, followed by a yelling baby.

"Could you pick Quentin up, Hon? I'm answering the door."

"I was changing his diaper. Who is it anyway?" Becca stepped into the front room wearing a Tokeca Community College sweater and jeans. An infant was bundled in her arms. Just outside the apartment door stood my sister. "Oh. Hi, December."

"Hey, Becca," she replied. Walking past me, she reached out to run her fingers over the child's head. "Oh, little Quentin. You're so cute. Can I hold him, Becca?"

"Of course, Aunt Deci can hold you," Becca declared. Tiny fingers tugged gently at her shoulder length strawberry hair. As December took the baby, I wondered why adults naturally spoke like oversized children in the presence of infants.

"I'll never get used to the idea that my fob brother is married and has a baby boy," December claimed, staring at the slender wedding band on Becca's pale finger. In baby-speak, she added, "Isn't that right, Mr. Quentin Nevsky Grazer?"

"Our big boy turns six months old today," Becca Grazer smiled.

"Really." December seemed thrown off by the news as she rocked the smiling lad. "It seems like you two just tied the knot."

"I thought women were good with dates. Try February 7th of last year," I reminded. "You're a little young for Alzheimer's, aren't you?"

"If I wasn't holding your kid, bro. Your arm would be sore right now."

"Why do you think I waited until now?"

Becca and December laughed.

"Your husband's a fob," my sister countered.

"Yes," grinned Becca. "But I love him anyway."

After a while, Becca went to the kitchen to make dinner while I followed *Aunt Deci* to the crib.

"I know you gave up on mysticism," December whispered, after setting her nephew down. After removing a little red cap, embroidered with a G, she placed a *Sonic the Hedgehog* blanket over his powder blue outfit.

"No, sis," I resisted. "Absolutely not."

"It's just that I gave the letter away," she confessed.

"You what," I barked.

"Is everything okay, guys," Becca called from the other room.

"Fine," December responded, seeing that I hadn't disturbed snoozing Quentin. Stepping into the hall, she continued. "Look, Hugo. There's a group, mostly Euro-based, that's recently popped up in some US cities. Dalton wanted it investigated but I told him no."

"And?"

"Well…he got Gypsie involved," she stated. "It's not a big deal. I sort of loaned…"

"Gypsie has the letter," I questioned as we stepped into the front room. Becca was there with *Totino's Pizza Rolls* and *Crystal Pepsi*. "Are you fobbing insane?"

"Now what's going on," asked my wife.

"Aunt Deci, here, gave the most powerful object in the universe to our fist happy sister."

"You didn't," Becca said, astonished.

"Universe? That's a bit extreme, bro," she claimed, removing an amethyst geode from her *Lee Rider* jean pocket. "Check this out."

Becca and I peered into the beautiful rock. The shifting brilliance parted to expose a city street. Cars were damaged and store fronts vandalized.

Three figures in black hoodies and leather gloves marched toward my brother, Dalton, and sister, Gypsie. Mannerisms and exposed skin revealed each as Caucasians in their early twenties. Two wore ski masks and dark safety helmets with an emblem; a dark ring outlined in white with the words *Not Us* in red and black. Their female companion, several pounds out of shape, had a bandana over her mouth and woodworking goggles.

From the violent acts in the background, I suspected the neighborhood was mostly African American. These members of *Not Us* were out of place.

The woman assaulted my siblings with hateful accusations but neither reacted. With little muscle mass, Gypsie didn't view them as a threat. Gogglegirl brought a small black canister from her backside and sprayed chemical in Dalton's face. Carrying wooden sticks, the trio rushed at them. Dalton got a mean whack on the head before Gypsie realized how serious the situation had become.

Seeing her brother's bloody head, she knocked the first man straight between the eyes. She followed the first move up by jumping into the air, spinning then kicking two skulls together. Safety equipment aside, the three were on the concrete.

"This happened in the beginning of May," December announced. "The riots had been well underway when *Not Us* arrived."

"This is in LA," Becca realized. "I thought this was about the black community and the beating of Rodney King."

"This group saw the chaos and took advantage of the situation," stated December.

"Why? What's their motive?" I considered.

"No one knows. That's why Dalton got involved," December said.

"What does this have to do with the letter?"

"Just watch," she insisted.

"Call me a Nazi," Gypsie yelled, stepping past the fallen woman. She'd shattered the eye protection and blood stained the torn bandana.

"There was only one oppressor on this street before I took charge, boys and girls, and it WAS you. Maybe change the name of your little club, fobs."

Grabbing his hand, my sister helped Dalton to his feet.

"You might be an okay politician, bro," she stated. "But as a fighter, you suck."

"Yeah," Dalton agreed. "I don't have your edge, sis."

"You never did," Gypsie laughed. Hearing her brother's sudden intake of oxygen, she turned. The fallen woman had lifted her body up onto toes and fingertips, glaring with eyes more akin to a reptile than human. With little effort, she brought the mass downward then thrust her horizontal body upward until her frame rotated vertically. Seeing the woman in a standing posture, Gypsie stepped in front of our brother. Fists came up in preparation for a fight.

The instigator kept her arms at her chubby sides. Her mouth opened to reveal an almost alien rasp.

"You Grazers need to leave well enough alone," she croaked. Like giant roaches, her male companions had sprung up and scurried onto a nearby business. As they crawled out of sight, she claimed, "The coven insists you back off before they are forced to step in."

The heavyset woman gravitated to the wall like metal to a magnet. Her fingers and feet carried her upward, facing my siblings, then onto the roof.

"The coven," I repeated as the image became a kaleidoscope of brilliance again. "Heart said she was taking charge."

"It doesn't sound like it happened," December said, putting her rock away. "Sorry, bro."

"I hope she's alright," I declared. "Either way, this is none of my business. If you think Gypsie needs the letter, then that's your choice. I'm a husband and dad now. My biggest drama should be diaper duty."

Afterward, we talked about everything from December's rock collection to the latest news in the war over Kuwait, even about a new public service they were calling the world wide web. Finally, I followed December to the front door. Turning, she placed an object in my right palm. It was a crucifix, made from a dark shiny substance, fastened to a leather cord.

"It's tourmaline crystal," she explained. "It's said to protect the wearer from minor maleficia."

"December."

"I know, I know," she insisted, stepping from the apartment. "But if you wont wear it for us then for Becca and Quentin."

"I love your family, Hugo," Becca announced after December had left. "But they all know you're not that guy anymore. Involving you is just an obstacle in our life together. Don't they see that?"

"Fob it! I've told them not to involve us," I insisted. "You heard me tell her."

"I don't think you try very hard," she remarked. "A part of you still wants to discover weird creatures and talk with the dead while I get the part that..."

"No, no, no," I insisted, gripping the cross. "I asked Zisk and DeMorney to keep the ghosts in the neighborhood to a minimum."

"You said you see them all the time," Becca said. "Can spirits be policed?"

"They said they'd try."

"I don't want to hurt you, Hugo," Becca claimed. "I just don't think you understand the profound consequences this has on us…on you!"

"I'm trying, Babe."

"I know that but…never mind. We'll talk about it some other time," Becca insisted but it was apparent that she was upset. "My mother's expecting us in less than an hour."

In the restroom, I hurriedly shed my clothes and got into the shower. After some warm water and teeth care, I put on December's gift. I got dressed then began combing my hair. In the mirror, I saw the sparkling black cross. The argument was still fresh in my brain. She didn't have to spell it out. As much as I wanted to believe it afflicted someone else, I knew exactly why Becca was bothered.

"I know we don't talk much," I prayed. "I just wanted to touch base and thank you for my wife, son, brothers, sisters, Mom, Dad, and all my friends and family. I really thought I was going to spend my life being beat down and eventually die alone. Thanks for proving me wrong, Lord. If it's not too much, could you help me avoid losing everything."

It wasn't *Matthew chapter six,* but I felt the *Man Upstairs* understood what I was trying to convey.

Regrettably, it didn't stop me from drumming up memories of that accursed nightmare. Worse, every time my wife and I argued, I wondered when elements would interweave with reality. Was Becca capable of the atrocity I saw in the dream? I didn't believe so but, still, something would attack my mind.

The strong version of myself departed, leaving

a frail Hugo. Fear stalled my mobility, making it harder to reach the restroom exit. What would happen when we left the house? Quentin?

Becca entered to find a grown man crouched next to the toilet. I was shaking and my eyes were red with tears.

"This is exactly why I don't like your family bringing up the supernatural," she said then gave me a hug. Words refused to come from my mouth. I had the image of the 1978 Chrysler Le Baron her father had given us as a wedding present. The moment I saw the fake wood and green interior, I panicked. It was the exact car from the dream. Other things clicked into place: Becca's hair, her makeup, clothing choices.

Becca took my hand and guided me off the floor. "No matter how much you fight it, a part of you thinks that dream will come true."

"Becca," I finally said, sobbing. "I don't want to believe it."

"You don't have to, babe," she insisted. "I checked the bus schedule. It'll be at the corner in twenty minutes."

That hadn't been our first argument. Becca Grazer had figured out a solution to my concern the moment she first saw that station wagon. No matter how intense the disagreement, the Le Baron stayed home.

You see; my wife wasn't that homicidal creature from my nightmare. She's Becca Grazer, the woman of my dreams.

ABOUT THE AUTHOR

Kevin W. Cousins considers himself a literary storyteller and created the following: ex-hi-bi-tion (also available in Audible), ex-hi-bi-tion More Shorts, the Larry the Spider series (Larry and the Creeping Horde, Bride of Larry, Children Shouldn't Play with Dead Larry, Larry the Spider Addition, as well as an illustrated adaptation of the short story 'Larry'), Second Chance Gate (an adult Christian tale), Crossing (2 parts), Bignose (an illustrated tale), and the Hugo Grazer Chronicles (1 through 10). Each is available through Amazon and Kindle. Kevin and his wife reside, modestly, in his hometown of Muscatine, Iowa. He is the father to an estranged son, a stepdaughter, and grandfather to her adorable children.

www.ingramcontent.com/pod-product-compliance
Lightning Source LLC
LaVergne TN
LVHW050549160826
845677LV00011B/2244

* 9 7 9 8 4 2 3 4 0 2 3 5 8 *